A Fist Full of Earth

by Pavel Kozhevnikov

DORRANCE PUBLISHING CO
EST. 1920
PITTSBURGH, PENNSYLVANIA 15238

Dorrance Publishing Co
585 Alpha Drive
Pittsburgh, PA 15238
Visit our website at *www.dorrancebookstore.com*

ISBN: 978-1-6442-6644-1
eISBN: 978-1-6442-6641-0

The Russian Hawaiian

To Uralsk Cossacks,
who were dispersed
all over the world
during the Communist reign in Russia.

Uralsk Cossacks - *a group of Cossacks in the Russian Empire located on the Ural River (now it is part of Kazakhstan). The earliest mention of them in history books is July 9th, 1591.*

Numerous books were written about the Uralsk Cossacks by great Russian writers and poets. Pushkin, Tolstoy, Krylov, Dahl, and Bushkov have highlighted that "they were not easy, these Cossacks. They loved freedom above all else. For the freedom and for their Christian faith, the Cossacks did not spare their lives…"

They were of different nationalities: Russians, Ukrainians, Jewish, Germans, Tatars, Kazakhs, Kalmyks, etc. Not only were enemies afraid of them, the central Russian power kept an eye on the Cossacks, suppressing their enormous uprising against tougher government control. After all, it was an island of democracy under the Tsar's nose.

Now the Uralsk region has the new "owners," who are performing all sorts of tricks, trying to distort the history of the Cossacks and their culture, although, there is nothing to fear. No troops, no Krug (government), and not many Cossacks are there. But there is the memory. The memory of these free and beautiful people…

With love and great admiration to my beautiful wife,
Gail Louise Kozhevnikov (Wilson).

There are so many fascinating and strange fates churning around us in this world...

A few years ago, my wife and I decided to go somewhere for Christmas vacation. We chose Hawaii.

After two and a half hours, an old Boeing 707 dropped us off in the make-believe movie capital of the world – Los Angeles. From there, we boarded an engorged cruise ship called *the Diamond Princess* and set out for our cruise to Hawaii.

The Diamond Princess was luxurious; everything seemed to cater to an elite minority. Despite the almost 3,000 people on board, we never encountered unruly crowds or lines. *The Princess* made her stops at ports-of-call on five islands where we took daily excursions, returning each evening to the ship. These hectic day trips occupied almost all of our time, not allowing for the enjoyment of even a short stroll through the natural paradise in this corner of the world. It bothered me so much that at the last stop, I went on strike against the *cultural tour* that I had already shelled out a small fortune for and determined to find a beach. My wife went on alone to get *culturized* and I stretched out under the sun to get a kick, or as we say in Russian, *to get kife.*

It got hot fast and I needed a drink. I had jumped into some shorts, threw on a Hawaiian jersey, and went to the little café I found that was nestled under a sprawl of leafy palms near the beach.

I didn't stay there long; the heat inside the café was suffocating despite the hysterical blowing of the air conditioner. I bought a bottle of beer and got out. There weren't any seats available outside under the umbrellas, so I decided to kick myself under a tree. I gazed out at the sea and realized that my selection of a beach had not been entirely successful. Hardly anyone was swimming. This was a beach for surfers.

The sea was tossing its tall emerald waves into the broad inlet to the very edge of the fine, gold sand and tall palms, behind which loomed fashionable high-rise hotels.

A group of young people were trying to catch the waves with small boards. In the distance, where the bay opened up to embrace the ocean with crushing waves, some of the surfers rushed out on white foaming peaks like trusty steeds, arousing great enthusiasm and envy among the poor tourists who were promenading on the jetty, sitting in the café, and lying on the sizzling sand.

Pretty soon, I was bored sitting under the tree, but going out onto the searing sand didn't seem like a wise decision. I felt that I was already sufficiently burned up, but still, I couldn't bring myself to leave that paradise. I saw a guy vacated his seat under the colorful Hawaiian umbrella and quickly moved there.

A waiter with an Asian appearance and a kind, inviting face appeared at my table. In strongly accented English, he asked me for my order. It was noon. It was hot. The humidity was so high that I had the impression if I waved the hand through the air, my palm would be dripping. I ordered a frozen rum daiquiri.

Directly across from me was the harbor. A pair of silver-haired Americans with unusually white and even teeth were sitting to the left of me. To the right, lying on the sand, were some large canoes. Behind those canoes near the café, there was the *Surfing Service* office, where from time to time, people were coming to rent and return boats. On the second floor of the building, there was a large restaurant that opened up to an airy veranda. To the right of the veranda was the balcony of someone's apartment. The balcony was covered in bright, tropical-colored ivy. I noticed a couple of times that a handsome, old man of average height was popping in and out onto the balcony. It struck me that he was Hemingway's late-aged look-alike. He looked out at the harbor through binoculars.

The waiter appeared with my drink.

"Do you happen to know who that man is?" I asked without any purpose.

"That's George. He owns that restaurant, this café, and that business," he answered eagerly, pointing to the *Surfing Service* office.

The waiter and I exchanged a few words. I learned from our brief conversation that he had come here from Malaysia looking for work. He liked everything about it here, everything was ok for him.

The beach was starting to empty out. I leaned the chair back and began to look at the ocean. Its waters had changed from their usual heavenly baby blue to nearly black when a rare cloud floated across the sky. A tranquil coziness came over my soul. As the soft breeze blew, I drifted into sleep.

I was awoken by somebody's attractive baritone voice that sounded near me. Somebody was speaking in Russian intermingled with English.

"Sonny, go and get that son of a gun! He doesn't know what the heck he's doing! Go and help him, otherwise he'll drown!"

With surprise, I opened my eyes and saw who was speaking. It was that older man who looked like Hemingway.

"Ok, Dad, I'll get him. Don't worry," answered a tall, bronze, good-looking boy. With a movement that seemed natural to him, he tied a surf board to his leg, lifted it with ease, and went into the water. While waiting for the next wave to break, he skillfully caught its retreat with the board and went out to the sea.

The old man watched his son for a minute, then turned to go to his office, but noticing that I was watching him with curiosity, asked, "How are you?"

"I'm well. Thank you, sir," I answered automatically.

Catching a light accent in my answer, this *Hemingway* asked, "Where are you from?"

"From Colorado," I answered with a smile, knowing that after it, there would be another old, familiar question.

I have a problem that I can't seem to get rid of my little accent. Those non-American soft consonants give me away. When I was younger, I spoke more succinctly, but as I have gotten older, I have been less vigilant, and my accent has started to come through more vividly. I stopped caring and trying to do better because, after all, my American wife loves such an "appealing Russian accent."

That's all fine and well, but sometimes I get tired of the same questions. You start talking with a stranger. At first, a stranger doesn't care about your speech, but then somehow, somewhere, I make a consonant too soft and immediately the stranger, like a rooster at the farm who hears human speech, stretches out one ear and then the other. Then comes the question, "Ummm, where are you from?" and my answer, "From Kazakhstan." Then there's a little confusion and then, "Where is that?"

Nobody knew about Kazakhstan before this idiotic film *Borat.* Usually in order to wrap up this barrage of questions, I answer, "It's a country between Russia and China," and then change the topic.

After the release of "Borat," it became much easier for me to explain where Kazakhstan is. Borat didn't assuage the ignorance of the vast majority of Americans in terms of world geography, but at least it helped them to acknowledge that a country called Kazakhstan exists somewhere. It looked like *Hemingway* was going to follow the same pattern.

"No, I mean where you from are *originally*?"

"From Kazakhstan," I answered with a smile.

"And where from, in Kazakhstan?" asked the old man with interest, switching to Russian.

"From a small city called Uralsk. Have you heard of it?" I asked.

The old man looked at me more attentively, then came closer and sat down with me under the umbrella.

"Have I heard about Uralsk?" he uttered with a noticeable quiver in his voice. "Not only have I heard about it, my countryman, but I used to live there many years ago! Only for me, it's not Kazakhstan, but the land of the Uralsk Cossacks," he said, correcting me.

Now it was my turn to be surprised. "Seriously?! Are you from Uralsk? That's fantastic! To meet a compatriot here in the middle of God knows where! Are you from the city of Uralsk itself?"

"Yes, brother! From the city itself! From *Kurini* – an old district there. The *Hemingway's* eyes became warmer.

"And what about you?" he asked, switching to the informal "you" in Russian.

"I'm from the *Selec* District."

The old man looked puzzled.

"Where is that?"

"You don't know where *Selec* is?" I asked with surprise. "It's seven kilometers to the north of Uralsk."

The old man looked at me with even more confusion. "Is that behind the *Belokazarma*?" he asked with uncertainty.

"Yes, it's on the bank of the Derkul River," I nodded. At this point, I was struck with a realization and I quickly asked him, "When have you been to Uralsk the last time?"

The old man smirked and wistfully answered, "A very long time ago, my brother, a long time ago. Not since….'41."

I was stunned by what I heard. I was anxious to inundate the old man with questions, but for some reason, I couldn't utter a single word. We kept silent. Meanwhile, a young, stout Hawaiian had come out of the office and said to the old man something in the local language. My *Hemingway* got up very quickly, and without any gesture whatsoever, went to the office. It was such a pity that the opportunity had just escaped from me to hear the fascinating story of the old man's life. That the story would have indeed been fascinating, I did not doubt for a second.

About ten minutes passed. The sun had moved past its zenith. It got even hotter. I was about to leave the beach, but at that moment, the same Hawaiian came out of the office, and coming toward me, said in pretty good English, "Excuse me, sir, if you have time, would you mind having a cup of tea with Mr. Freedman?"

I was surprised and asked, "Who is Mr. Freedman?"

"He's my boss. He just talked to you."

I understood that he was talking about my *Hemingway* and I very quickly agreed. We went through the office and up to the second floor. The Hawaiian knocked reverently on a door that displayed a bronze plaque with the word "Private."

The door opened, and the old man had already changed into a short-sleeved white shirt and khakis, smiling, said, "Come on in, brother. I see you're not in a hurry, and I also have a free hour. Besides, it's time to get a bite to eat. Do you mind?"

I didn't mind. The ship was supposed to leave in the evening. My wife was on her excursion and so I had plenty of free time. The old man led the way, inviting me to follow. We went through a couple of rooms, one of which seemed to be the living room and the other his office. Everything was furnished simply but elegantly. In the room that looked like an office, because there was a desk and all the walls were adorned with books, the old man had opened up some French doors and we ended up on a spacious balcony with an ocean view. It had been on this very balcony where I had noticed *Hemingway* for the first time.

"You may take a seat here," the old man said, pointing to a bamboo arm chair.

I sat down at a small table on which there was a beautiful Venetian crystal vase full of fruit.

The old man made himself comfortable across from me, and smiling again, said, "Welcome, my countryman. Let's get acquainted. My name is Lebedikhin Yegor Pavlovich."

"Then who is Mr. Freedman?" I asked with surprise.

"That name is for *them*," he said while brushing his hand to the side dismissively. "When I got tired of hearing how they butcher my name, I decided to become George Freedman. As you might know, Freedman means *free man* and the word Cossack also means *free*."

"Well, it's a pleasure to meet you," I replied.

It was my turn to introduce myself. The old man listened carefully to my story, and when I finished, he asked, "Well, what shall we have to eat?"

I shrugged my shoulders. "Well, what do you have to offer?"

The old man burst into laughter. "Anything you wish. I own this restaurant and so my chef will prepare whatever you want. Do you want *vareneki, pelemeni, golubtsy, borsch*? You won't find these things on the menu, but my chef knows how to do Russian cuisine and usually whips up something tasty for me."

"You know, I would like to try something local, if you don't mind," I answered.

"No problem," he said and went out to place the order.

He returned rather quickly, and within five minutes, our table was overflowing with different varieties of dishes.

"We're going to drink vodka, right?" the old man asked assumingly.

"If you don't mind, I'll just have some white wine," I replied, feeling a little guilty.

The old man looked at me with surprise, threw up his hands with irritation and pretending to scold me, saying, "Russians are getting soft. They don't even drink vodka anymore!"

"Oh, no, we still drink, but today, it's too hot for vodka," I tried to justify myself.

"Yeah, yeah, just my point. Like I said, you boys are going soft!"

This "boy" was already over 50, but I decided not to argue. Instead, I smiled in a similar way, threw my hands in the air, and jokingly said, "You're right, we're just shitheads!"

The old man laughed sincerely. Bottles of vodka and wine were brought out to us.

"Well *Pasha*[1], let's drink! It's my birthday. I turned 81 today. God himself has sent me, not only a Russian guy, but a countryman on this day. If I were to tell somebody, they wouldn't believe it! Come back tonight with your wife or with whomever at ten o'clock. We'll take a trip into the mountains where I have a luxurious villa and we'll party all night long."

"Sorry, George, by then we'll be far out at sea. But thank you so much for the invitation!"

The old man winced as if he had swallowed something bitter. "For you, I'm Yegor. If you prefer, call me Gora, just anything but George!" he said, gumming it. "It's too bad you can't be my guest. Well, let's celebrate it now," and to my amazement, he decisively moved my glass of wine out of the way and put a full shot of vodka in front of me.

---

[1] *Pasha* – diminutive of Pavel

I gave up. "Oh well, Yegor Pavlovich," I said, (I could not bring myself to call him Gora in such a familiar way) "allow me to offer a toast to your health. May all your wishes come true."

The old man grimaced again.

"No, Pasha," he interrupted. "We're not going to drink to my honor. I'm ok. All my wishes are in the past. Instead, my countryman, let's drink to our Russia. Even though she has thoroughly crapped into my soul, the Motherland will always be the Motherland, and every human being has only one, just like we have only one mother. You cannot hate her! Especially since now I hear that Russia has gotten onto the righteous path."

We clanked our glasses and drank. Everything was exotic and delicious. I concentrated mostly on the seafood. The old man ate very little. Instead, he was reflecting on Russia's place in history. Then suddenly, he started asking about Uralsk, Kazakhstan, and Russia.

We were already finishing the first course of food when he suddenly made an out-of-place remark, "I guess I still have relatives in Uralsk. My parents have passed away for sure. Even though we have longevity in our family, they would be over 100 by now. But my younger brother, Petro, could still be alive. He's by now…about 75-years-old."

"You haven't been home since the 1940's?" I asked with surprise again.

"No, Pasha, and I don't want to. The Gulag is not for me."

"What do you mean, Gulag? All of that is in the past, Yegor Pavlovich," I exclaimed. "Times have changed."

The old man grinned. "Maybe the times have changed, but the KGB is the same. I know what they're capable of, Pasha!"

I shrugged my shoulders with disappointment but didn't contradict him. We drank another shot, then ate a little something and sat for a short while in silence. Then the old man spoke again.

"Pasha, I know what you're thinking. I see you looking at me with reproach and wondering how I could have forgotten everything, my mother, my country; how come I didn't send a single letter and didn't go to visit. But what do you really know about my life?"

I was getting nervous that this conversation might become like Vladimir Vysotsky's song, *Captain, You'll Never Become Major*[2] and so I decided to change the topic and asked him about Hawaii.

The old man carelessly answered something, and then with some guilt in his voice, said, "Sorry, Pasha, for being curt. I don't like digging up the past. I have always tried to avoid soulful, nostalgic conversations and all that crap. But today is a special occasion. You, my compatriot, and from Uralsk on top of it! Here in Hawaii, it doesn't happen very often. But what am I saying here, not very often? In all my years of being here, this is the first time it has happened. So, my fellow countryman, let's don't rain on our parade. Instead, let's drink to us, to Cossacks. Without us Cossacks, there would be no Russia in the first place. Cossacks – this is the strength of that country!"

The old man looked at the ocean and said, "I don't like weak people. All my life I hated them. That's just how I am – just like my mother used to call me, a good-for-nothing! Since childhood, my spirit has been innately risky and rebellious. In our district *Kureni*, I was the head of a local gang of urchin boys. Back then, I was always starting some shit, or as they say nowadays, 'leading.' But to tell the truth, I always made good grades at school. Literature and German came especially easy to me. I was naturally strong, very strong. My fists were made of steel. I remember one time we went to swim in the Ural River. It was a Sunday, it was hot, and there were a lot of people. So, we were lying on the sand, sunbathing. I was about 16-years-old. Suddenly, we heard screams and noise. I looked around and saw a big, bullying drunk creating some commotion. I saw him punch one guy, then another, and

[2] *V. Vysotski* - a famous Soviet poet and actor. His famous song, *Captain, You'll Never Become a Major*, tells about the conflict between fathers and sons.

both of them were knocked out. All of a sudden, a small man appeared out of nowhere, trying to calm him down. Right behind him was his wife and children. I'm thinking that's the end of this guy! This big bully is going to embarrass him in front of everybody. My heart sank just as the drunk grabbed the little man by the arm and was getting ready to punch him. I jumped right behind the big jerk and lightly pushed him in the back. He turned around with surprise, and I saw his drunken eyes were filled with rage, and pushing the small man aside, he lunged toward me. I didn't do anything special, I just instinctively stretched my arm out, so that my fist was right in front of that bulldog's muzzle. That giant toppled over as if he was broken in two. Everybody gasped, and for a moment, a total silence descended and then they all started to praise and admire me. The little man, the one whom I had sort of rescued, was totally stunned by what he had witnessed, shook my hand, patted me on the shoulder, and kept calling me a boxer. Meanwhile, the drunken giant got up without much understanding as to what had just transpired, started cussing, and right at that moment, the militiaman appeared. And so, the big thug, I and two witnesses were taken to the militia station. Thank God it was right next to the beach. Then all the paperwork started. The witnesses described everything as it had happened and even presented me as if I was some kind of hero.

'Look, that's what exercise can do! Take a look at this young guy. What a huge man he took down! So, where do you study boxing?' the little man asked.

That irritated me. 'I'm not a boxer.'

'You're not a boxer? So, if you're not a boxer, where did you learn to fight like that?'

'I didn't study anywhere. I just have a very heavy hand,' I said and shrugged my shoulders. Then I turned to the militiaman and asked, 'Comrade Militiaman, can I go now?'

'Get out of here, Lebedikhin, but no more fighting!' he answered sternly.

'Thank you very much, of course, for your intervention; however, to punish violators of the law is the duty of the militia and not of those who have strong fists. Otherwise, we will end up with the mob law.'

I left the building without knowing whether I should feel happy or sad. I had walked just a little way before the small man caught up with me and said, 'Listen, lad, if you're telling the truth that you have never studied boxing, then it means that you're a natural-born boxer and so you're absolutely obligated to start taking boxing lessons! You'll become a champion, I tell you! And don't be upset with that militiaman. He's very young and inexperienced, it makes him overzealous. I've given him a reprimand.'

I didn't know what it meant, *to give him a reprimand*, and looked at the small man with curiosity. He abruptly stopped, extended his small hand, and introduced himself.

'My name is Ivan Petrovitch Kalugin. Come to my place of work tomorrow,' and then he gave me the address. 'I'll give you a note to one outstanding coach. He will turn you into a true champion.'

I nodded my head and hurried back to the beach. I immediately forgot about the whole conversation. But what do you expect? I was just a kid," sighed the old man.

We took another shot and he continued.

"So, I finished high school, and as soon as I had started working at the factory, the war began. Just like all my friends and peers, I ran out straight away to enlist, hoping to get sent to the front. All of us at that particular time were crazed with patriotism that was bubbling out of us like champagne out of a bottle. We completed a quick physical and then had three days to get ready. At the factory events center one evening, the management had created a special farewell gathering for us. Everybody was in a good mood as if we weren't really going to war. We all thought that we'd punch Hitler in the nose, and then three to four months later, would be welcomed back home like heroes. Basically, we really bought into Stalin's motto: *We are going to fight the enemy on his own territory*. May that bastard be three times damned!"

The old man opened a box with expensive cigars. "Want one?" he asked me.

"No, thank you, I don't smoke," I answered politely.

"Good for you! And I cannot refuse this pleasure when I drink. My favorite cigars are Cuban. It's the best of what that country has to offer. Though maybe not. Women over there were also excellent but maybe now such women have become extinct. This mother fucker Castro rounded up everybody and put them in barracks." The old man lit a cigarette, inhaled, and closed his eyes.

I was afraid at this point he would stop telling his story, so without holding back any further, I asked him, "So, what happened next?"

The old man opened his eyes and looked at me attentively. It seemed he was flattered that I was interested in his narration. He pleasantly smiled and continued.

"All of us boys went out to dance for the last time before we shipped out. The events center at our factory was very small. At the beginning of every public event, there was the obligatory, solemn Communist ceremony. On the stage, the party leaders were giving fiery speeches and shaking our hands and the like. When the gramophone finally started playing, the chairs were removed and we began to dance. There were so many people that we couldn't even breathe. On each side of the dancehall near the walls, there were two busts. They were positioned on top of something red that I can't remember. They were the busts of those sons-of-bitches: one of Lenin and one of Stalin. They were staring directly at us, as you might understand, with that strict Commie glare!

At that time, I had a girlfriend named Tanya, Tanyusha. She was a dark-haired beauty – a real Cossack girl! She was terribly in love with me. And so, when *the White Dance*[3] was announced, she invited me, but I didn't know how to dance a waltz. She started teaching me and there were, as I said before, so many people like sardines in a can. We were just dancing shoulder-to-shoulder. Somebody accidentally pushed us, and we crashed directly into that Commie shit – right into Stalin! It's only nowadays I can say that about him, but back then – he was God! There was a lot of noise and Stalin broke into pieces. The music stopped. The crowd receded with fear. Some were in a hurry to run out of the dancehall, and me and Tanya just froze as if we were paralyzed and didn't know what to do. I came out of my stupor first. I grabbed her by the hand and ran, naïvely thinking that we would get away with it…

Right! As if good fortune would fall out of the sky. I was arrested the very next morning.

They took me to the *NKVD*[4] and interrogated me. At first, everything was quite civilized. But soon after, they really beat me in earnest. They tried to force me to sign a confession admitting that I had broken the bust because I hated Stalin. I refused to sign it, trying to explain how it had really happened. After each refusal, they beat me again, and they beat me with relish! After a few days, they took me to some kind of office where a man in uniform was sitting at a table. When he dismissed the armed escort who had brought me and lifted his eyes to look at me, I recognized that little man from the beach.

Eventually he recognized me, too. He read the paperwork, listened to me, and sadly shook his head, saying, 'You're in a world of shit, Yegor. You're looking at a minimum of 15.'

I somehow inappropriately shrugged my shoulders. Kalugin – I re-

---

[3] Sadie Hawkins dance.

[4] *NKVD* – Russian abbreviation for the Peoples Commissariat for the Internal Affairs, predecessor of the KGB.

member his last name as if it were yesterday – got up and started to pace slowly back and forth in the office. Then suddenly he stopped, looked into my eyes, and said, 'I'll try to help you. I believe that you did not do it on purpose, but it's way too late to try to prove anything and on top of it all, your girl isn't exactly testifying on your behalf.'

I winced. Seeing it, Kalugin was in a hurry to calm me down.

'Don't judge her. We make everybody confess. You see, she's only a girl, she probably didn't phrase something right, or maybe we just didn't ask her the right thing, but at this point, it doesn't really matter.'

When he saw that I was impatient to give my objection, he stopped me by lifting his hand and saying, 'Now they're going to take you away, and I will think about how to help you.'

Just before calling the armed guard to take me out, he suddenly asked me, 'Why didn't you come when I asked you to before?' I shrugged my shoulders with guilt.

'Oh well, keep your chin up. Everything is going to be alright, I think,' and he patted me on my shoulder.

Yeah, he helped me alright! Instead of 15, I got seven! But I guess I should be thankful for that. I have never seen him since. I was locked up for two years before I got "lucky." They sent me to the penal battalion. I don't think there is any need for me to tell you what it was, a Red Army penal battalion, do I?"

I nodded my head, signaling that I understood.

"That fucking war shook me up, Pasha, just like a bull does with a shitty bullfighter. I was wounded several times, but everything healed up like on a dog. I didn't even go to the hospital. I don't know how I survived that meat grinder. I thought, just a little more time and they would pardon and transfer me to a regular platoon. But no! At the end of '44, I was captured by Germans. A mine had exploded and deafened me. I had lost consciousness from a concussion, and when I came around, the Germans had me surrounded. Then there was the concentration camp. I escaped and was caught again, and again, put back in the camp, but this time, I was sent to a camp inside Germany itself. What I experienced there, I never want anybody else to experience. I got lucky in 1945. I was liberated by our troops. We were all as happy as children, but our happiness quickly evaporated. Our soldiers fed us, let us get cleaned up, and then the officer came and ordered to lock us up in barracks only to drag us out, one at a time, to a special interrogation unit. Well, I knew things weren't looking too good. When I was still on the front, I had seen how our boys who had escaped from the German camps would come back to us with tears of joy in their eyes. But then they were either sent to the penal battalion or executed. Since I was already coming out of the penal battalion, I knew quite well what was in store for me."

The old man lit his distinguished cigar.

"In a word, Pasha, I ran away from my own kind and wound up in Bavaria on American territory. Unlike our people, the Americans believed me and helped me out. I think I probably wasn't the first one to show up in the same situation. So, I ended up in America in New York. The first couple of years were hard but then I picked up the language and got a job as a taxi driver and things improved.

One event helped me and changed my life dramatically. I was driving along in my cab in the New York night, and while passing by one of the parks, I saw three scummy guys beating up a nicely dressed man. I don't know why I stopped my car though; I had a client in it and jumped out to help the poor fellow. Right away, I took two of them down, but the third guy was stronger than the others. It took me a little more time to mess around with him, but in the end, I took him out, too!"

The old man's eyes brightened with a youthful energy. It's as if he even got younger just telling me about that incident.

"I got a little bruised up, too. My lip was cut open; my eye was black – in a word, a real beauty! The man whom I saved didn't even thank me for rescuing him, but instead, with an expression of fear, stared at me like he was trying to memorize my face and then he disappeared. I got back into the cab, excused myself to the customer, and drove off being angry with myself that I had interfered in that mess. Suddenly, I heard the voice of my customer, a very firm and confident voice. 'You're a pretty good fighter. Are you a boxer?'

I looked into the rearview mirror. The client was well dressed and seemed like the well-bred sort.

'No, I'm not a boxer.'

'Where did you learn these hooks?'

Briefly, I told him my story. I don't know why I did it. He had a way of making me feel comfortable. I felt that he took an interest in me.

It turned out that he was the owner of a big restaurant that had an indoor boxing arena where there were fights on the weekends. Those fights, in nowadays terminology, were freestyle!

'Listen, son. Come to this address,' and he gave me his business card. 'You may ask for Sam Brown, that's me. I think you could be a very good fighter. Of course, we have to work with you a little, but if you're not lazy, you'll earn good money. A lot better than you do now driving this cab.'"

The old man filled the glasses again. The telephone rang, but he ignored it and continued his story.

"This time, I didn't miss my chance. The very next day, I went to see Sam. This American turned out to be a very good man. He was a former boxer himself of medium height, his face was covered with scars; tough, even sometimes severe, but fair guy. He helped me out a lot in those first days: loaned some money, found a room not far from his restaurant, and included me in his team, which he himself sponsored. There were about 15 men in the team. Our coach was a freckle-faced Irishman. I was a quick learner making fast progress. Then my first fight came. The opponent was some red-headed Scotsman. I looked at him, thinking I would knock him out in the first minute. There were a lot of people watching it, and almost all of them were betting on the redhead. Nobody knew me at the time, and he was, as I found out later, not a newcomer to this business. Well, I got into the ring and… froze. The lighting, the shouting, the clouds of smoke shocked me. My hands and legs became like cotton as the redhead beat me up with all of his might, making hamburger out of me. The referee had to stop the fight two times. I was given medical help. I tried to punch but failed to even graze him. My assistant was that Irishman. Sam was sitting on the first row with a calm poker-face, sipping whiskey.

Finally, when I was totally covered in blood and had gone to sit down in my corner after one more lost round, he came to me and asked, 'Well, George, should we throw in the towel?' and even though spots were floating before my eyes, those words touched me in my soul and I grunted out, 'No, boss, I will fight!'

Sam kind of nodded his head in relief.

'Ok, son, then stop jumping around, and don't be afraid of him. Imagine yourself out on that street where you beat up those jerks. Imagine there's no crowd here, nobody but you and him, and catch him when he moves toward you. He's left-handed. I noticed that when he hits with his right hand, he usually punches two times. Then he follows up with a left-hook and that's his ultimate blow. But before the left punch, he opens up completely and it's at that moment when you need to catch him. Ok?'

Sam uttered those words very quickly. As he admitted to me later, he didn't think I had understood anything he said, but I got everything. The main thing was that I stopped being afraid of the crowd and their awful whistling and heckling. Following Sam's advice, I imagined myself one-on-one with that guy somewhere on the *Kureni* street, and immediately, the power and reaction returned to my body.

The last round started. Sam was right, that redheaded guy opened up his body like on schedule, right before the left punch. A couple of times I tried but missed. Finally, on the third time, I got him. I crushed him with all the strength left in me, with my right hand directly to his chin. The blow was so strong that the redhead collapsed, sliding down the ropes onto the floor... The crowd in the arena gasped, then shrieked, and fell silent. They were stunned! Nobody had expected this turn of events. Then shouts, whistles, and applause. Somebody was assisting the redhead, someone was holding up my hand, and then someone was carrying me into the dressing room.

Sam walked in happily, congratulated me, and said that he needed to go watch a couple of fights and told me to sit tight. I took a shower, put some bandages on my cuts, poured a little sparkling water for myself, and sat in a cozy armchair. For the first time in many years, I felt happy.

The fights were over. Sam summoned us to his restaurant, not to the regular dining room, but into one of the separate, luxurious, and well-furnished smaller rooms. The day for Sam had been very lucky. Out of the five boxers he had put into the ring that evening, only one had lost. The money circulating around in that business was pretty significant. Because of me, Sam was a big earner that night. Nobody else had apparently bet on me. And so, we ate and drank some lemonade. Alcohol wasn't allowed. It's only in all these new-fangled movies they show now the boxers get drunk after each fight. That's dog crap – a Hollywood invention. The scripts for those Hollywood films are written by kids who are wet behind the ears and don't have the faintest idea what real boxing is"...

"Well, my brother, let's throw back one more shot. Since we're talking about it! Let's drink."

We drank, and I was starting to feel a little tipsy. I definitely liked this old man.

"You're not tired of my tall tales yet?" he suddenly asked, turning his face to me.

I looked into his eyes and was struck by their lively, youthful strength. It seemed to me that his recollection of those events from long ago made him anxious but younger. I believe he wasn't really telling the story for me, but more to himself, as if he was recounting, justifying the meaning of his life, summing it up.

"No, not at all! I'm not going to leave until I get to hear everything right to the very end," I rushed to assure him. "Please, go on, it's so interesting!"

I didn't lie; the story of the old man truly carried me away with its extraordinary and colorful picture of the encounter.

The old man smiled and continued.

"When the dinner had come to an end, everyone else left, but Sam asked me to stay.

'Well, young man, congratulations on your maiden voyage,' he said while stretching out a hundred-dollar bill. That was big money in those days. I took the cash. Sam got up and patted me on the shoulder.

'Good job! You're a real hard-ass! Today, you gave me the bare minimum. But you're not quite ready for a real fight. Roger the Blacksmith, or even someone else on a lower level, would eat you for lunch. Let's start working in earnest. Your punch is a gift from God, but you're a slow-mover and your stamina is weak. There is nothing to worry about it, that's not too hard to correct. From now on, I'll train you myself, separate from the rest of the group.'

I looked at him with surprise. 'You will train me?' I blurted out.

Sam gave a slight grin. 'Yes, I train. Why, son, are you surprised? I only work with the most talented. Five world champions started their career with me,' and he named them.

So, he started training me and I mean to tell you that he was a real macho man! He grilled my ass so much that I nearly hated him, but he made a real fighter out of me. I fought a lot of fights. I not only beat Roger the Blacksmith but many others. Of course, some of them beat me, too. Well, Pasha, life got really interesting. Suddenly, there was easy money, friends, and women. There were lots of girlfriends, but all that sleeping around was just a shallow pursuit, so to speak. I had everything I could ever want, so I started to drink out of boredom. You should never give too much to a Russian man, because of his fragile soul, he'll wind up spending every penny on booze…

Sam tried to reason with me, tried to convince me of my unique traits and talents that he said only appeared once in a lifetime; he even yelled at me, tried to persuade me, but all was in vain. His patience eventually ran out and I ended up on the streets. Like us Russians say, Pasha, *I went through fire and the water, but the brass pipes cut me into pieces.* Pretty soon, my money was all gone and then nobody needed me. I had become…what is that new English word in Russian language now?"

"A loser?" I prompted.

"Yes, yes, that's it, a loser! I was as low as low could get – less than zero. I lost weight, let my beard grow in, my hair got long. I spent nights in places you can only imagine. One time, I woke up in a dump beaten so severely that all my ribs were broken, and I was covered in blood. I had a foggy recollection of the day before, all drunk and getting into a fist-fight with some hoods. I remember the beginning of the fight, but then I think somebody cold-cocked me from behind with something heavy. They threw me in the damp and left for dead. I crawled out with my last breath toward the nearest street and collapsed onto the pavement. But Lady Luck smiled down on me. The black guy who found me and picked me up was the same guy whom I had defended from a gang of thugs on the street before. He was a nice, cheerful man. He lived with his mother and a sister named Michelle. She was beautiful. Her skin was almost white, her big, black eyes covered half her face, but the thing I really remember was her hair. You know, only mulattos or Italian women have such thick, voluminous hair…

But when Jim – that was the name of the black guy – carried me home, I was so incoherent that I didn't notice anyone's beauty. For one week, I existed between life and death. Their mother was a powerful woman. The energy in her spewed out like a fountain. She was blacker than black. Her teeth and the whites of her eyes were blinding. Her name was Rosalinda. She went to work early in the morning and came home very late. She worked in some hotel as a laundress. She had the hands of a wrestler. I found out only later that she had been against me staying with them in her apartment – she didn't like whites. But when she found out that I had saved her son's life, she started to treat me like a son. As soon as I had somewhat recovered, she gave me a lecture from hell! I knew I had to stop drinking. It was difficult – a real nightmare. Only former alcoholics know how tough it is to quit. But I'm a Cossack! In a word, I got myself together and went cold turkey. A semblance of normalcy returned. It was time to find a job.

Michelle worked in a restaurant somewhere. She usually got home very late and left very early, so I rarely saw her. Jim got by with the occasional odd job; sometimes he would sell something, sometimes he would give somebody a hand, but regardless, he always had money in his pocket.

And so, I began looking for a job but nothing worthwhile came up. Mother, as I started calling Rosalinda, used to laugh and calmed me down. Her favorite expression was, 'Welcome to America!' I was not happy about that and scowled.

A month or two passed, I don't remember. Whatever I was able to bring home was earned by accident, and when I tried to give it all to Mother, she would refuse it by saying, 'You're a man and you have to have money in your pocket,' or 'Once you find a permanent job, son, then you'll start chipping in to the family budget.'

One time, Mother told me that they were looking for a loader at Michelle's workplace. I was ecstatic! Early in the morning, Rosalinda woke us up and we went to the interview.

The restaurant where Michelle worked was not too far. It was about a 40-minute walk, but we were in a hurry and took a bus.

I remember it was chilly and terribly windy. Basically, it was a typical New York February. As Michelle and I walked to the bus station, we were silent. She was wrapped up in a long coat that covered her from head to toe. She wanted to go to the bus section for colored, but I decisively walked her into the 'white zone.' At that time of day, there weren't very many people in the bus, and those who were there did not pay much attention to Michelle. In any case, it was almost impossible to know that she was actually a black girl.

We arrived and walked into the restaurant from the back door. Michelle pointed out at the office of the manager and left. To make a long story short, they gave me the job. The work was not very hard, and the pay was miniscule, but at the very least, I stopped mooching off of my black Mother. I got a new change of clothes and came back to life.

I would go to work with Michelle, but afterwards, I usually returned alone because she was staying there very, very late. Sometimes she even spent the night there.

As I already mentioned, Michelle was really pretty. Rosalinda had probably messed around with an Italian guy because Michelle looked more Sicilian than black. The whites were checking her out, and for some reason, I liked it. The relationship between Michelle and me was close, similar to the relationship between brother and sister. It stayed like that right up until an incident that changed our lives forever.

Spring arrived, the trees were flowering, the air was practically streaming into my soul, giving it some kind of ethereal lightness. I felt that my entire body was filled with a pleasant, bouncy strength. I wanted to love and be loved. I wanted a cheerful, bright happiness.

One day, I decided to take a walk after job. The streets were full of couples and romance. You can always tell those couples that are in love just by the way they walk, by the warm, tender looks and by their grace-fulness, especially when it comes to the young women. My happiness slowly turned into a light sadness. I felt that I was totally lost in this huge concrete jungle. I turned around to go into the subway and took a shortcut through narrow little streets, so I could avoid looking into those happy faces.

Suddenly, right in front of me, I saw an amazingly beautiful woman and something about her seemed familiar. I had approached her and wow! It was Michelle standing there and talking with a huge dude. They were arguing about something or other. I said hello to Michelle; she startled and stood still for a second before grabbing me by the hand to pull around the corner. The big guy cussed us out while we walked away.

'Hey, girl, you only have five minutes! The client won't wait!'

When we had gotten about ten paces away from him, Michelle jumped all over me with anger.

'What are you doing here?! Are you spying on me?!'

I was really surprised with such a turn of events.

'I was walking home and didn't even think about spying on you! But you, what are you doing here?'

I'm not going to recount our entire conversation-fight, but when I realized she was not working in a restaurant whatsoever but instead 'ser-

vicing clients,' then I got as mad as a bull and grabbed her by the hand, forcing to follow me.

Michelle did not expect such a development and began to scream and resist, but I was extremely strong back then. I wanted to take her away from this evil place, help her, save her! I swear that in that particular moment, I was only feeling a brotherly kind of love.

Suddenly, I heard the big guy whistling and two other gigantic men just like him jumped on me. I understood that there wouldn't be any way out of this without a fight, so I positioned myself with my back against the wall of a building. Michelle tried to stop them by explaining that I was her brother. They started laughing hysterically.

'This shit is your brother? Bitch, you sure you ain't blind?!'

'Guys, don't touch him. He'll get out of here right away!' she cried, trying to shield me with her body.

The big fellow slapped her in the face with his greasy hand, and as she fell, I noticed that he had a gun in his hand. I could not wait any longer – I hit him, and with a moan, he was stretched out on the concrete. I threw one more punch and the second guy slapped down on the ground right next to him. The third guy, after seeing all of that, ran for help. I kicked the gun to the side with the toe of my boot, and grabbing Michelle, headed toward the subway.

Not too far from our apartment was a small park where we sat down to catch our breath. Michelle was completely shaken. I gave her a hug and held her against my chest as if she was a little child and I comforted her.

'Calm down, sister, everything is ok. Nobody will ever touch you again, I swear it!'

She pushed me away, her eyes flaming with anger, and beat me in the chest with her small fists.

'You don't understand what you have done. You screwed everything! They will never leave it alone now. There's a whole gang of them! They're going to kill you! Why did you do that?!'

'Michelle, I only wanted to help you, I saw that you were in danger. I don't want you to make a living like that. You're worth more than that!' I said, trying to explain myself.

'You're an idiot! It's not your business! Who are you to tell me what to do? Because of you, I lost my job!'

'Michelle, I'm your brother – I am in debt to your family, to Rosalinda! And what if she were to find out?'

'Find out what?' she screamed. 'That I am a prostitute? Fuck you! She already knows!'

I was stunned. I got up slowly and wandered away aimlessly in the direction of my stare. She caught up with me and was saying something, apologizing, crying, hugging me. I don't know how it really happened, but I could not restrain myself and I kissed her on the lips. She jerked back and burned me with her enormous eyes. I thought she was going to hit me, but instead, she unexpectedly embraced me. We stood like that for a long while, listening to each other's heart beat and I felt, Pasha, that there was not any other woman in the world more precious to me, and that is how I fell in love for the first time in my life…

There was a huge chasm between us. We were completely different people, different in upbringing, culture, language, and most importantly, I was white and she was black. Only recently have things become simpler, but back then in the 50's, blacks weren't even considered human, and for an interracial marriage, you could go to prison or even be killed. Simply put, everything was against us. Only blind love was our 'ally'."

Suddenly, a knock on the door had interrupted his narration. The waiter walked in, apologized, and served us dessert. The old man grew somber, unhappy that he was forced to leave his memories behind and return to the present moment. He poured a shot of some expensive brandy into small golden shot glasses. We took a drink and he continued.

"Michelle was afraid to come back home that night. The big dude knew where she lived. Michelle said he was very revengeful and never forgave anybody for disrespecting him.

We got a room in a cheap but clean and tiny hotel. While Michelle was taking a shower, I ran to a nearby store and bought some food, whiskey, and stuff like that. As I was entering our room, I saw Michelle standing nude in front of the mirror, brushing her hair. It took my breath away. I was standing with my bag of groceries near the door and couldn't move. It was as if I was chained up by some power, amazing and unknown before.

She turned and approached me. Believe me, Pasha, I was afraid. I had seen a lot of women before her, but I had never seen such a beauty! I could not have imagined that the female body could be so gorgeous... We merged into each other and were wild until the morning. Even now I thank God in my prayers for that wild night...

In the morning, we went home. Michelle made me wait in a small café and told me not to come with her because she was afraid for me. She came back fast. It turned out that she was right. Those gorillas had come to Rosalinda's that very evening, beat her up, and then waited for us all night long.

As soon as I heard about it, I wanted to punish those bastards, but Michelle stopped me. It turned out that those guys were just little pawns in the big machine of the criminal underworld that included cops and the Italian mob.

Michelle and I had some bucks. We rented a small apartment in one of the boroughs of New York and started looking for a job. These were the happiest days of my New York life. During the day, we ran away crazy while looking for any job we could find, but the night was ours. We were madly in love with each other and forgot about the world around us.

But the world soon reminded us: we ran out of money and still didn't have a job. My mood turned serious. Michelle saw it and was worried about me. One time, she came back home in a good mood with a bag full of food and drink. I figured it out immediately, and we got into a huge fight. I tried to leave and maybe I even slapped her in the face. She cried, fell to her knees begging and justifying herself. She told me that she did it without any feeling, that it was just mechanical. She was afraid to lose me and wanted to make me happy. I believed her and decided not to leave. But I told her that if she ever did again, even one more time, there would be nothing left between us.

I said all that but knew this couldn't go on, and I began thinking about where to find big money, so that Michelle would never need to sell herself again.

Help came in the form of Jim, her brother, who sometimes came to visit, giving us news about Rosalinda and all their neighborhood.

When I expressed my desperation to earn money for Michelle's happiness, he listened carefully, then looked at me and said, 'You know, George, if you're serious about it, then I have a proposal for you,' and he shared with me, as it seemed to me then, a long-thought-out plan. The offer was nothing less than robbing the money couriers at some supermarket. He explained his plan in detail.

I listened to everything Jim had to say and saw that he had really thought it all out, down to the last detail. The job was risky, but it had pretty good chances for success. What did I have to lose anyway? At that time, I was often pondering the unfairness of life, especially seeing all the wealthy people around in their luxurious limousines, mansions, and offices. What a pity that I, a strong and healthy man, was totally unable to find a job, forced to endure a pitiful existence, while those *fat cats* were living high on the hog and didn't even know how to spend their money sums of which were so grand that they wouldn't even have missed a million or two! This is how I justified myself back then, so I quickly took Jim up on his offer.

He introduced me to a street-smart Hawaiian whose name was Hilo. He was taller than average and had obviously been around the block a few times, having been through the hell and high water of the New York slums. Hilo was a bottomless pit of energy and optimism. All three of us discussed the plan in detail. I even took a ride out to that place and was convinced that it was doable.

Essentially, the plan went like this: in that busy store, money couriers take the earnings at exactly five o'clock. A big, black car pulls up next to the store (back then, stores didn't use armored cars for the transport of money like they do today). From that car, two well-armed money couriers get out while the third one, the driver, waits in the car. They approach the office through a small service door not too far from the main entrance of the store, which for some unknown reason was never locked. Behind the door, there's a long, wide hallway and a few offices. In the middle of the hallway is a small vestibule with two doors to the bathrooms, in one of which we decided to hide. Within exactly ten minutes, the couriers leave the office with the money and pass by the vestibule. Jim and I had the job of neutralizing them. Hilo's job was to grab the bag as quickly as possible right out of the hands of one of the couriers. There was only one man missing in our plan and that was the one who would wait for us around the corner in a car, so we could make a quick getaway.

We could not trust anyone outside of our immediate circle. Not to mention the fact that we didn't want to share our take with anybody else. We frantically began thinking about how to solve this problem.

Of course, we could have tried to execute the plan all on our own, but the parking lot next to the store was just a little too far from the entrance to the office and was usually crowded with other cars, making it impossible to get away without being noticed right off the bat. So that left only one possibility. Somebody would need to wait around the corner of the building with the car running. Temporary parking with a running engine was allowed at that place.

Suddenly, Jim suggested Michelle as the getaway driver – as it turned out she knew how to drive a car. I was resistant for a long time but Jim, without my knowledge, told his sister everything. At first, she was angry and didn't want to hear about our escapades. Then out of the blue, she agreed! She liked the idea of us finally being able to get out of New York City to build our life somewhere upstate. Her only condition was no killing. She started talking me into it. In the evenings, she would be dreaming aloud how everything would work out, how we would buy a house, what kind of furniture, how many children we were going to have, and so on and so forth. I was grudgingly sucked in and agreed. Naïve? Yes, we were young and naïve. We wanted to be happy, and we were willing to pay any price for it…

The day arrived. We pulled up to the store in a car we had previously reserved under an alias. The car was old but reliable. Michelle stayed in the car with the engine running.

Everything happened so fast. The couriers arrived, got out of the car while the driver stayed put, and they went into the store. I, Jim, and Hilo followed them. The couriers were walking through the hallway with loud footsteps and disappeared behind the doors of the office. We entered the men's bathroom and began to wait. I was calm and slightly opened the door to keep my eye on the hallway. Jim and Hilo were noticeably nervous. Minutes dragged by painfully slowly. Finally, I heard the door being opened and the money couriers exiting the office and heading toward us. The sound of their footsteps was menacing in the empty hallway. I began to worry, too, but I wasn't worried like one of those shaking cowards who quiver all over and lose control; I was worried like you worry before a fight in the ring, when your entire body is filled up with lead and you're ready to go to battle. When the money couriers were just a few steps away, I came out of the bathroom. My appearance did not surprise them at all – they were big, strong men and armed.

As they came toward me, I knocked one out with a short right hook. Following my lead, Jim jumped on the second courier, but that guy had time to kick Jim off his legs and grabbed the revolver. He did not have time to use it before I punched him in the jaw with all my might – it cracked, and he fell down onto the floor like a sack of potatoes.

Hilo pulled out all of his lock picks and somehow, doubtingly, started digging at the lock that handcuffed the courier's hand to the money bag. I noticed how Hilo's hands were trembling. One minute passed, then a second, and still, he was picking at the lock.

Suddenly a door to one of the nearby offices opened and out stepped an ugly fat lady. Realizing all that was going on, she started screaming, shouting 'Robbery! Help! Call the police, somebody!'

The doors to other nearby offices started opening up, too, and frightened faces were peeking out from them - just one more minute and we're done! Jim grabbed the gun and shot a couple of times into the ceiling and then all the doors closed. Finally, Hilo got the handcuffs opened. I grabbed the bag and we ran toward the exit.

Jim is running out first and bumps right into the third courier, the driver, who after hearing the noise and shots, was rushing to help his comrades. Suddenly, there was a loud shot and Jim falls down dead. The driver points the gun at Hilo, but I just have enough time to knock him down. I'm passing the bag with the money to Hilo, throwing Jim on my shoulders, and we are rushing toward the idling car around the corner. Behind us was a serious chase, we hear screams and curses, we run toward the car, I push Jim into the backseat and collapse right next to him. Hilo with the money bag jumps into the front seat next to Michelle, and we are riding really fast through the narrow New York streets. I turn around to see that there is a cop car on our tail and behind the wheel is a fat cop. Michelle is not one of the best drivers, but she is pushing the gas pedal to the maximum. That helps us lose the tail, but suddenly, Michelle notices that Jim is dead and letting go of the wheel, starts screaming. Hilo slams on the breaks. The car lurches to a stop, almost hitting a pedestrian who immediately disappears.

Michelle is jumping out of the car totally confused, trying to get pass me to Jim. I cannot calm her down. From around the corner comes the fat cop's patrol car. I am pushing Michelle into the backseat next to Jim and sliding behind the driving wheel with the pedal to the metal. The tires are spinning out and smoke is literally flying out from under them. In the rearview mirror, I have just enough time to see the fat cop get out of his car and aim at us. In the next second, the bullets busted out the windshields, I hear them whistling right past my temple. Again, we lose him and drive into ghetto. Hilo is sitting down, pale, pushing the money bag up against his chest. It's quiet behind us. I am turning around and immediately slam on the brakes. Completely pale, without any blood in her face, Michelle is trying to stop the bleeding in her chest, and her entire hand is covered in blood.

'Why did you stop? Go! Go!' Hilo is screaming into my ear.

'Shut up! Don't you see she's wounded?!' I shout wildly back at him, crawling out of the car and opening the back door. Michelle's huge black eyes are looking at me with surprise.

'George, my love, I am dying,' she whispers with a shaking voice.

'No!' I am screaming like a madman. I'm tearing open her blouse and under her small breast, slightly below the heart, I see a gaping wound from which blood is pouring out.

'Hold on, Michelle, hold on, I am going to help you right now,' I am telling her as quietly as possible, and tearing my shirt, trying to dress the wound.

Hilo is standing paralyzed next to us. Somewhere not too far on a neighboring street, we could hear the sirens of police cars.

'Busted! We need to book it out of here!' Hilo says while grabbing me by the arm.

'George, my love, run! I am done for anyway! Leave me be!' Michelle moans.

I turn toward Hilo and scream and order him, 'Run, Hilo, run, buddy! I cannot leave her!'

'No, brother, we'll run together! She's right, leave her here! They will have to help her. Hurry up, man! We've got to get out of here!' he shouted while trying to talk me into it.

'Run I told you!' I was crying. 'Maybe you'll end up living a normal life for all of us. Run, you motherfucker!'

Hilo steps away from us reluctantly, I see tears in his eyes and then I see him dash away and disappear around the corner, holding the bag against his chest.

I lift Michelle up and run as fast as I can toward the sound of the police sirens..."

The old man stopped talking. It seemed to me that he was silently crying. But in a minute, as if regaining consciousness, he lifted up his blue eyes toward me and they were dry. But the blue in them had become darker.

"Pasha, let us drink to Michelle, to my first love, let her be an exquisite memory!"

"Did she really die back then?" I asked clumsily, then immediately understood the stupidity of my own question.

The old man smirked, crossed himself, and took a shot.

"Yes, she died in the hospital. When I ran in front of the cops and laid Michelle down in front of them, they put in handcuffs on the spot and shoved me toward the cruiser. I turned around, Michelle was pale, but even more beautiful than ever, she moaned, 'I love you, my Russian,' and fainted.

I howled like a beast, tried to break free, but one of the cops hit me in the head with a baton and knocked me out...

Later on during the investigation, I found out that Michelle had passed away on the surgeon's table."

The old man got quiet again. Fearing that I would not have time to listen to this amazing story to the end, I rustled him out of his deep thoughts.

"And so, what had happened next, Yegor Pavlovich? What happened to you next? Did they ever find that guy, what was his name, Hilo?"

"No, they did not find Hilo, and so, what's next? Next, there was a trial, and I got ten years. They could have given me the max, but I was lucky. I had a very nimble Jew lawyer that rewrote the entire history and presented me as a victim of love. 'After all, my defendant could have just run off with the money, but instead, he stayed behind to save his love.' I think that's how he wrapped up his closing argument. He blamed everything on Hilo, portraying him as some monstrous mafia hood. At the trial, I found out that there was a lot of money in the bag.

Throughout the investigation, Rosalinda visited me every day. I once tried to apologize to her for bringing so much pain into her life, but she stopped me, saying, 'You know, son, my children are in better hands now – they are up there with God! All of us, you, me, we all sooner or later will be there. And you will meet your Michelle again and be with her forever...'

She was very religious, that wonderful woman! But it doesn't matter how you turn it all around in your mind, you cannot command your heart, and people like Rosalinda have hearts that are pure and big but easily wounded. Rosalinda passed away soon after trial…"

The old man took a deep breath, lit a new cigar, and continued.

"I served my time in its entirety and then got out. The first thing I did was go to the cemetery. I cried there, I brought flowers to Mother, to Jim, and to my Michelle. What I felt at that moment, I cannot even tell you! You know, I didn't even want to go on! I thought back then that I should end all this mayhem called life… What time is your ship leaving?" he asked suddenly.

"At 10 o'clock," I answered, looking at my watch. It was already 6 o'clock in the evening. The sky was overcast, and it was getting cooler.

"I just don't want you to be late," smiled the old man.

"Don't worry, Yegor Pavlovich, my wife is supposed to come back from her excursion at 7 o'clock. She'll call me on my cell," I answered.

"Alrighty then, we can continue a little more relaxed," he replied and poured some more brandy into our shot glasses. We took our shots and he, seeing my impatience and desire to hear the story through, asked, "Where did I stop?"

I helped him.

"Yes, I was standing at the edge of an abyss, Pasha. No job, no money, no home. I was dreaming of Michelle every night, she was beautiful and desirable. It's those stupid thoughts that were swarming around in my head, so I decided in all seriousness to end my life.

I thought for a long time how to accomplish it. During the day, I would walk around, begging and pan-handling, and think about it. I would go to a shelter at night, eat whatever I was given, lay down on my mattress, and think, think, think. Basically, in a few words, I decided to jump off the bridge. I'm not sure why, but at that particular time, it seemed like jumping from a bridge would be easier than jumping from a skyscraper and splatting onto the sidewalk.

I was searching for just the right bridge for a long time and then I finally came upon the highest one possible. One late afternoon, I headed out toward the bridge to settle the score with this perverted life.

I found myself alone with my thoughts on a back street, thinking about this callous, incoherent life for the last time. I walked and walked before I noticed that I was lost and couldn't find the bridge. I knew New York City extremely well because, after all, I used to drive a cab there, but I didn't recognize that neighborhood. In my daze, it seemed like I had wandered into the wrong place.

Suddenly I noticed a small Orthodox church with signs in Russian! At first, I was stunned. How would a Russian church end up here? Then I recognized it. Once upon a time, I had dropped off a passenger here. I silently smirked and said to myself, it looks like God wants me to say a prayer before the departure.

I walked into the church, and since I wasn't in any particular hurry to get anywhere, what would it hurt to say a prayer just in case. I was not very religious back then, but I wasn't an atheist either. It was cold, autumn weather outside, but inside the church, it was warm. The candles were burning dimly; the smell of incense hung in the air. The church was dark and seemed empty. The last, thin ray of the setting sun was shining down on a huge icon, hanging over the pulpit. I don't know why, maybe I thought this would be my last prayer, but I got down on my knees and whispered, 'God, forgive me for all my sins, I'm a loser. I know that I decided to do something unholy and so I am not asking for your blessing, I am asking for forgiveness. I cannot go on living in this world! This world is obviously not made for me, forgive me, God!'

I continued to pray. But it wasn't a prayer but rather a clumsy and confusing confession of sins. Toward the end of it, I opened my eyes;

by this time, they were used to the dark, and with fear, I noticed that I wasn't alone in the church. Not too far from me in the corner stood a small man in a black cassock and was praying. I got up off my knees and slowly went toward the door.

'My son, hold on!' said the man, paralyzing me with his low and handsome voice. I stopped, and we began to converse. They called him Father Michael. He had come to New York in the wave of post-revolutionary immigrants. His father had also been a priest in Russia, but after he was shot by Commies right in front of his son's eyes, the young man and his mother ended up in China and then made their way to America.

Father Michael was a true man of God. He possessed amazing appeal and friendliness. We went into his small office and I told him my story. I'm not sure how it happened, maybe he hypnotized me, but I felt better from this short, unexpected confession. To my surprise, Father Michael didn't try to talk me out of it, he didn't try to insert sense into me - he just quietly nodded his head and crossed himself.

Later, as if he had forgotten about our conversation, he started talking about something else: about good and evil, about his parishioners, about the Russian diaspora, and about how difficult it is to maintain his church. I was bewildered but listened to him, surprised and even slightly stunned by his worldly occupations at such a critical time.

Suddenly he turned his face to me and said, 'Listen, my son! I see that you have been thinking about executing a bad and ungodly plan, but I don't have the strength to stop you – only God is your judge! Since this is the end, do me a favor and help our church.'

'But what can I do, Father, to help the church?!' I asked dismayed. 'I don't have any money. Everything I own is just the shirt on my back.'

'We don't need money, what I'm asking for is really ordinary. We could do it all by ourselves, but most of my parishioners are old and infirm,' he said with slow restraint. 'The heating of the building only works sporadically, and we need to dig a trench for the new pipes. The old ones are below the wall and you can't get to them. The backyard is so small that no equipment can get into it and we're looking for anyone who can help us out. You won't have to dig; we'll find someone else to do that. You'll need to haul the bricks that are lying over the place where we'll need to trench. Find another place to move the bricks to; it shouldn't take more than about three days of work. In the meantime, you can lodge and eat with me. And then do as your soul tells you to do. God is your judge.'

I couldn't say no. The very next day, I started carrying bricks, carefully stacking them next to the wall. In the evening, Father Michael came for me, and we headed to his small house next to the church where I spent the previous night. We ate a modest meal and talked.

At the beginning, he was the one who did most of the talking while I listened, and then, I got carried away as if a bomb exploded! I was erupting with all the anger that had accumulated over the years - anger against the world, people, and myself. Father listened to me without interruption. I squeezed all the bitterness of life out of me and began to feel relieved, as if all of life's splinters were removed from my soul. And I felt at that moment, with all my heart, that there is a God! I felt ashamed for all my wrongdoings, for my entire misspent life. I was crying, and with each tear falling from my eyes, my soul was cleansed of its sins.

I couldn't sleep that night. I was remembering and pondering my whole life. The next morning, I worked with renewed vigor. Toward the evening when the last brick was stacked, I went to say goodbye to Father. I entered the church where the liturgy was taking place. I stood up next to the parishioners and crossed myself and would you believe, Pasha, something holy and pure swept through my soul unlike anything I had ever experienced before.

When the liturgy ended, I remained standing like I was in a coma. Father Michael approached, we walked outside, and I asked him, 'Maybe I can help you with the trench?'

'No, my son, go into the world to live. I see that you are healing, but it's still too early to meet your Creator in heaven, you have not walked your entire path on this earth yet,' he said.

I didn't understand what he was saying at first; in my work and in our conversations about God, I had forgotten all about my decision to commit suicide. Father Michael had cured my soul! How he accomplished this, whether through hypnosis or through a true spiritual intervention, I do not know, but I left him as a completely different man, totally changed. We hugged each other firmly like brothers; he prayed for me and I walked into a new life.

I passed a few neighborhoods, put my hand into my pocket, and there was an envelope with money. I understood immediately that Father Michael had succeeded in putting some money into my pocket during our farewell. I was so moved that I almost started to cry. It was only a little bit of money, but it greatly helped me in my time of need.

I rented a small room in the suburbs, and shortly thereafter, found a job at the port. It was really hard work; hauling bags of sugar that were shipped from Hawaii. But the money was good. Little by little, my life began to fix itself; new friends, new clothes, and once, I even visited Father Michael. He was not at the church, and so I walked toward his house through that familiar backyard where I had been stacking bricks. I saw one downtrodden guy was carrying a stack of bricks back to the place where I had first taken them from. I approached him and asked what he was doing. The gloomy guy lifted his face toward me and he seemed ghostly, sad, empty, unearthly eyes - an exact copy of myself when I had been carrying those same bricks in that place. I knew exactly what was going on.

I found Father Michael, hugged him, and repaid the money he had given me – and even significantly more than what had been put in my pocket in my moment of desperation. At first, he refused, but I thrust it into his pocket with force and said, 'Take it, Father Michael, take it, summer is coming, and the church will possibly need new ventilation instead of new pipes.'

He realized I had discovered his *secret*, and with smiling eyes, he blessed me and went back into the church. I have not seen this holy man since...

Life went on. I thought that surely it would have no more surprises in store. But no, it looked like life always made an exception for me!

And so, toward the end of summer, the factories in Hawaii went on strike. There was less work and our crew, while waiting for the next shipment, was cleaning the warehouse that belonged to the company. On one of those days the supervisor arrived and called me and three other strong guys to carry some new furniture into our boss's office. The furniture had been bought a long time ago and was just gathering dust in the basement while the old office was being remodeled. The boss was named Mark Goldman. I'd heard a lot of good things about him. The workers respected him for his honesty and professionalism, but I had never personally met him until then.

We arrived in his office, carried the furniture in, set it up, and wiped the dust off. We were about to leave when a short man with clever, brown eyes and a big, open forehead came in and started shaking hands with everybody, giving each one of us an envelope with money. I looked at him and tried to remember where I had seen those eyes. I had a good memory for faces, but names elude me, faces, never. When he shook my hand, he inspected me, and I saw he also was trying to place his memory back. I thanked him and headed toward the exit. Suddenly he asked me to stay behind.

Everyone else left. He asked my name and where I had worked before coming to his company. When I mentioned that I had been a taxi driver, he suddenly lit up, jumped toward me, and began shaking my hands, looking into the eyes, asking, 'Do you remember me? Do you remember me?'

I was a little confused and casually answered, 'No, sir, I don't, but it seems like I've seen you somewhere before for sure.'

And that's when he reminded me that he was the man whom I had saved from those hooligans on the streets of New York when I had met Sam, the owner of the sports club. Indeed, he was that son-of-a-gun who had run away without even thanking me.

He apologized for his actions sincerely, sat me at the table, and opened a bottle of expensive whiskey. I liked him for his simplicity and honesty. He didn't try to come up with justifications, he just simply confessed that he had been afraid for his life and that's why he bolted away. But since then, he had been troubled by the fact that he had run away without even thanking me.

At the end of our conversation, he abruptly offered me a position as his personal driver and bodyguard. His business was growing, and as he put it, he needed some strong and loyal guys. I was flattered by such an offer, but before agreeing to it, I revealed everything about my past: that I am Russian, that I was in prison, etc.

He burst laughing, 'So what!? You're Russian, so is my wife. And prison? Not a problem. I was inside once, too, for participating in a Communist meeting. It's all history, look at me now! I'm a capitalist, hate Communism, and I love a Russian woman. Show me the man who has a squeaky-clean past!'

I started to laugh, too and agreed.

The job wasn't difficult, but it took up all my time. I became a part of his family, and for comfort's sake, he put me up in his luxurious mansion into one of the small but tastefully furnished rooms for the servants.

Everyone treated me nicely - everyone except his wife. In the beginning, I liked her very much, an impressive, hot brunette. Her name was Sofiya, but everybody called her by her American name – Sophie. She was from somewhere in Ukraine. During the war, the Germans snatched her back to Germany, along with many other young women from the occupied territories. But after the war, she, like so many others, went to the West. There was nobody in Russia, no relatives, and she didn't want to go back to that Commie shit.

Mark met her on the streets of Paris when he was a soldier. He was from a very rich family of Christian-baptized Jews, and even though his grandfather had fled the imperial pogroms somewhere in the western Ukraine, his grandson Mark strangely harbored a love and respect for everything Russian. That was one of the reasons he loved Sophie, I think. And, of course, she was beautiful. But she did not love Mark. And it wasn't because of the 20-year age difference. Mark was a good-looking, even handsome man, everything about him was pleasant, but still, she didn't love him and that was for sure. She didn't even try to hide it, snapping at him and creating fights over everything. Basically, he irritated her with his goodness, or maybe with something else - who really understands women? Mark acted like he didn't see that, gave into her every whim with tenderness and love.

At first, she didn't pay any attention to me. There were lots of Russians in New York back then and some of them worked for Mark. But one day, at Christmas, they went out to a restaurant. There were a lot of expensive cars in the lot, everything was lit up, and music was playing. I just barely found a place to park. They got out of the car, and I turned off the engine and went toward a group of other drivers who were playing cards near a fire not too far from the entrance.

Three hours later, I noticed that my boss was leaving the restaurant and waving me down. I hurried to him. He smiled awkwardly and asked me to take Sophie to the house, explaining that she wasn't feeling well.

I followed him into the lobby, and next to the coat check, I saw Sophie sitting down, drunk out of her mind. I don't even know how she got herself to the coat check. We put her into the car, and Mark told me to take her home and come back for him. He couldn't leave with her because there were a lot of very important people in the restaurant. For Mark, business was everything.

And so, I brought Son'ka (this is how I called her behind her back) home, lifted her up into my arms, and carried into the bedroom. She was totally unconscious. I laid her down on the bed and went to fetch the maid, but she had gone home for Christmas. I didn't know what to do. I couldn't leave her like that, fully dressed on the bed. I thought that maybe I could gently take off her clothes and tuck her in without her noticing or knowing who had done it. I started to undress her, trying not to look because she was so pretty. By the time I had taken her shoes and dress off, I was covered in sweat. I tucked her in and covered her up with the blankets, and suddenly, she regained consciousness and in uneven tone of voice, asked me in Russian, 'What's your name, handsome?'

'You know I am George,' I answered, startled.

'No, what's your real Russian name,' she asked.

'Yegor,' I answered.

'You mean Zhorik,' she laughed.

'No! Yegor!' I answered more firmly and turned away from her.

'Ok, alright, then I'll call you Gora, the mountain.'

I didn't say anything, so I could get out of there.

'Wait, Mountain, don't leave. I'm feeling sick. Help me get into a shower,' and that wicked woman was smiling in a whorish way.

I knew where she was going with this and I said, 'Sophie, right now, the most important thing for you is to go to sleep, and in the morning, you can take a shower.'

'Hey, listen, what's your name, Gora? Come here! Don't put on airs! Don't you see I need a man!' and she threw the blanket off of herself stretching herself out seductively like a big cat...

I couldn't even think about betraying Mark like that; Cossacks aren't those kinds of people. The Tsar himself had even proclaimed that the Uralsk Cossacks were the most trustworthy people in his environment. So, I turned around and left.

From that moment on, Son'ka hated me. As they say, *hell hath no fury like a woman scorned!* She started to create a lot of trouble for me. Then she began to falsely accuse me of things, demanding Mark to fire me. But Mark, who usually always listened to her, was very firm, 'Honey, leave this man alone! I need George!'

One time, when I overheard one of such conversations about me, I was forced to tell Mark everything about that night. Much to my surprise, it didn't upset him. He just smirked.

'Don't worry, she's a little crazy. I know about all her escapades and all her boyfriends. She wants something that I cannot give her,' and suddenly he began speaking in very good Russian. 'Give her what she wants, and she'll stop,' he said.

I froze. 'Mark, you know that she betrays you and then you're even asking me *to put horns on your head*?!'

'What does it mean to put horns on the head?' he asked with a purely American hunger for details.

I explained to him that it means to make a fool out of a husband.

'You know, my friend,' he said quietly and strictly, switching into English. 'I love her very much. She's my first, last, and only love. She's everything to me, and these indiscretions are not her fault. The war damaged her psyche. I don't wish her experiences on anyone. I bet you got through the hell like she and can understand it.'

He was silent for a while, and then looking through the window, he added with sadness, 'Time heals all wounds. I haven't always been a saint either – I did some terrible things but that's all over now. I think in time she will also give up all this wickedness in her and only the good shall remain. Don't judge her too harshly. Give her the benefit of the doubt. But thank you for telling me, just do your job and don't pay any attention to Sophie.'

I was stunned with his declaration. I never thought it would have been possible to forgive a woman like that. When I left his office, my masculine pride was fuming and howling like a wolf in the steppe. But after I calmed down a little, I remembered how Father Mikhail had once recited a passage from the Bible to me, where Jesus saved a prostitute and shamed those who tried to persecute her.

I didn't get any sleep that night. I thought about life, God, people… Mark for me had become like a saint, and after that, I started to look at life differently and was more restrained and more careful in judging others. Sophie eventually stopped pursuing me – a new gardener appeared, a young, handsome German.

Meanwhile, Mark's business was growing, and he started to travel around the world and usually took me with him.

Some years passed by and then the economy took a bad turn, Mark's business began to suffer. He became nervous and started to drink.

One summer, we flew to Hawaii. At that time, these islands weren't tourist destinations but just sugar plantations. One of the sugar refineries was there on the island. Do you see that wooden arm running from the hill to the sea not far from the dock? That's the actual remnant of the plant where Mark and I were at that time. The workers' strike was happening at this plant on top of all the other plants that

Mark owned. The workers were demanding an increase in their salaries. Mark really took the strike to heart and was suffering over it. Contracts were broken, and Mark's losses were sizeable. With that situation at hand, he had to figure out what to do in order to get his plants back up and running.

We stopped at a hotel near the ocean. During the day, I would accompany Mark to the plant, and at night, I was on duty in the conference hall where he would have meetings with acquaintances or trade union leaders. Negotiations were difficult. Mark was out of sorts; I had never seen him like that. Bankruptcy was looming.

After three days of negotiations, it was a stalemate. Mark got drunk to drown his sorrows and then decided that he wanted to go out somewhere and was trying to get to my car keys. When Mark wouldn't listen to reason, I did my best to calm him down, but he pushed me in the chest, lunged at the car keys, jumped in the car, and slammed on the gas pedal. He disappeared into the darkness at a crazy speed. I was standing there, just paralyzed. I took a taxi to go in search of him but didn't find.

I stayed awake all night, sitting in the foyer, waiting for Mark. When the police showed up, I learned that Mark had been killed in a car crash. They interrogated me for a long time, wrote their report, and went away. I called Son'ka to give her the news. She came from the continent with her "Hans." She was quiet and organized everything so quickly and then sent the body back home to the continental United States. Then she hired some local lawyer who eagerly began liquidating Mark's debts and sugar business. I tried to talk her out of it, but she didn't want to hear anything from me. Before her departure, "Hans" showed up and handed over an envelope with a severance pay and some official documents declaring that I no longer worked for her. I decided against protesting it. Maybe that was the best outcome for both of us anyway.

I took a little rest in Hawaii. The landscape was outstanding, and I felt like I had lived there all my life. It was like a paradise, warm weather year-round, ocean, seagulls...

The hotel where I stayed with Mark was too expensive, so I decided to find something cheaper, and very soon, I met a widow who rented a small room in her house right on the beach. I paid her for one week – that's how long I wanted to be there. I tried to forget about the world and started to let go a little - the sea by day and restaurants by night.

Time was flying. A couple of days before my scheduled departure, I noticed a beautiful Hawaiian girl in one of the bars. She was with a guy who never left her side. It was obvious the guy had money. His clothes, gold rings on every finger, thick chains – and by how the people respected him - I understood that he was a local 'authority'. I didn't care about his 'big show' and decided to ask the girl to dance. I was good and drunk and saw her sitting, looking bored.

So, I walked over and asked her. At the next table, friends of the guy went totally silent. They all turned to him, waiting for the order to tear apart this reckless intruder.

The girl looked at me with interest and suddenly smiled. Her suitor didn't even look at me but just carelessly flicked his hand dismissively, letting me know to get lost.

Even louder and more persistently, I repeated my invitation. And that moron jumps up and winds his arm back to punch me. I slapped him lightly and knocked the guy out. The guys at the next table jumped up to beat me, but the threatening shout of that beautiful girl stopped them. I couldn't tell what she was yelling in her language, but they froze and sat back down on their chairs and stared at me with pouty hatred. Some of them helped the guy to get up. That small 'navel' came to himself and pulled out a gun, but she told him something strictly, and glaring at me, he left the restaurant.

I turned to the girl with surprise, and smiling, remarked, 'Thank you very much, my beauty, for your persistence, but I'm used to paying my bill all by myself,' and I stretched my hand out to her and added 'Will you grant my wish and give me a dance?'

She raised up her eyes, and I immediately drowned in them. 'Well, *cousin*, you can't imagine how expensive this dance could be for you,' the Hawaiian girl said laughing and put her gentle but strong palm into my hand.

We started to dance. Her name was Mona. I asked about her boyfriend. It appeared he really was a rich guy. His name was Johnny. Johnny was her brother's friend who was the owner of the restaurant where we were now dancing. And I found out that Johnny loved her very much, had proposed marriage many times, but he would always be seen as her childhood friend and so she always turned him down.

When the music was over, Mona started to go home. I suggested to see her off, but she just smiled and said that the person who should be escorted home was me and pointed at the menacing group of guys who were standing by the door.

'While you are with me, cousin, there is nothing to be afraid of,' Mona smiled. 'So, let me take you to your hotel, or if you want, to the airport right away.'

'Running away after seeing you, my beauty? Not at any price,' I smiled, taking her arm and going out. The girl said something again to the guys, and the crowd parted as we went out onto the street. Then she caught a taxi and delivered me to the widow's boarding house. I tried to hug her, but she didn't allow it.

'You know, guy, I'm not joking, it's really better for you to run away as fast as you can. Johnny won't forgive you. I saved you today, but they're not afraid of me, they're really afraid of my brother. In my presence, they won't do anything, but tomorrow, you'll be alone, and nothing will stop them. So, gringo, you'd better get out of here as fast as you can.'

I protested, saying I'm not afraid, babbling on. She looked at me with sadness and shook my hand and turned around in order to get back to the taxi.

Unexpectedly I took her by the hand, pressed her to me, and kissed her lips. She flared up with rage, and with such surprising strength, escaped my embrace. I sensed that I had really offended her, and I suddenly regretted it. But the next moment, she looked from inside the cab and presented me with a funny little smile.

She rode away. I was left standing and following her with my eyes. For the first time in many years, I felt that the ice in my soul left by the loss of Michelle was melting...

The next day, I went to the beach in a really good mood, thinking about Mona. The sea was gracefully quiet, the beautiful palms smiled at me, the sun was shining brightly and gaily. I had swum out pretty far when, suddenly, three small motor boats surrounded me. The people in the boats were armed, and they ordered me to climb into one of the boats. Resistance was futile, and I obeyed.

One of the guys bound my hands so quickly that I didn't even have a chance to react. I felt a strong blow to my head and lost consciousness. I came to myself from a bucket of cold water being poured over me by one of the short bandito-type squab and found myself on the deck of a luxurious yacht. Some strange people were surrounding me. In the center of the crowd, men dressed up in white suits were sitting in the chairs. I couldn't see them very well because my face was covered in blood, my hands were tied, and my hair was matted up over my eyes.

I understood that I got into such a situation from which I hardly would get out. But it was weird; in my soul, there wasn't any fear or panic, I smiled to myself and thought, 'That's all, Yegor, enough of screwing around in this world.'

'Ha! Look at this ball-sack! He's still smiling,' I heard the voice of the man who was sitting in the middle of the table.

'So, Gringo, you are that insolent man who dared to raise his hand against my brother?'

The man who was speaking was obviously the leader among them, and his voice seemed familiar. He said something in Hawaiian and they put me on my feet.

'Well, Gringo, you offended my brother, which means you offended all of us here,' the loud shouts of agreement and whistles forced me to wince.

'You acted very, very bad, dude. I don't forgive such things. For such an offense in our land, there is only one way out – death! If you want to say something for the last time, then speak!' and I heard him cock his pistol.

'Well,' as carelessly as I could, I said, 'if the law in this land is to kill people for acting like normal men but not like cowards, then go ahead and shoot, but before I die, allow me to pray one last time.'

The guys around me were mumbling and jeering; the leader also laughed and said, 'Go ahead and start praying right now, here, you have three minutes,' and again, his voice forced me to flinch and concentrate my memory, but the recollection betrayed me, I could not remember to whom that voice belonged.

'Untie my hands,' I asked.

'What for? You don't know how to pray without hands?' laughed the guy.

'You can kill me, but why are you making fun of me?' I was mad. 'I'm Russian, and I need hands to cross myself before death. Are you afraid I'll run away?'

My last words were drowned in cackling. I shrunk myself and prepared for the worst, but out of the blue, someone came to me and re-moved the matted hair from my eyes.

'Wow, what a meeting! Is that you, George?'

I couldn't believe my eyes; Hilo was standing right before me!

'Hilo!' the only word I could pronounce.

Hilo gave me a strong hug, and to the surprise of the group, or-dered that I be unbound. Then he was saying something in Hawaiian, pointing with his finger to my chest. I saw how those people surround-ing us started to look at me with surprise and then admiration. I guessed Hilo was telling them about our adventures in New York.

Suddenly I saw Johnny sitting at the table with a huge black eye. He was the only one not laughing and looked at me with an alarming hatred, barely containing himself. When Hilo noticed it, he told him something harshly, and Johnny got up without looking at anybody and went into the yacht.

'Don't be afraid of him, he's an alright guy, and when he gets to know you better, you'll become fast friends. Nobody will ever touch you again, even with a little finger; this is my world, George, and I rule it,' Hilo uttered with pride and took me to the stateroom in his yacht.

The Lord saved me once again…

That yacht had everything. I got myself together, changed into the clean clothes that Hilo had given me from his wardrobe (we were ap-proximately the same size), and we sat down to celebrate our meeting. I told Hilo about my life and he about his. He appeared in Hawaii a while after we separated. First, he dropped out of life with all the money, then he managed to get to Los Angeles, changed his identity, and only after that was able to get back home.

We spent the whole day talking about old times. Hilo was really happy to see me.

In the evening, he gave me a hug and said, 'Joe, brother, everything

I have now is because of you. I never forgot what you did for me in New York and that's why I think of you as my own brother. A good part of my business today is yours! If you want to be my partner, I would be only too happy. If you would like to split it, it's also not a problem.'

I thanked him and said that I needed time to look around. We stopped there. He found me a deluxe room in the best hotel on the island, gave a car and driver and opened up a bank account for me. He also recommended that I rest, not to limit myself in anything, and then in a week, he would come meet me and we would discuss our plans.

I spent the whole week on the beach and never even went into the city, and even though Mona was constantly on my mind, I did not go looking for her. After my chance meeting with Hilo that had saved me from a savage outcome, I knew that he had trusted me and to break that trust was no good. I didn't know who Mona's brother was, but I didn't have the guts to ask Hilo. Exactly one week later, Hilo called me and invited to visit him in the mountains. I arrived at an exclusive estate with palm trees, servants, and so on. I was escorted to a nice big room where a lot of people were already. Hilo came out of the crowd in a snow-white suit and introduced me to his girlfriend, a slender Japanese woman. Suddenly the door of the room opened and out came Mona!

My jaw dropped, and my heart was pounding.

'Meet Joe, this is my sister, Mona.' Hilo kissed her on the cheek, then turned to me and winked, 'But I forgot that you already know each other.'

Mona came to me bravely and gently smiling shook my hand. She wore a beautiful blue dress. Her bronze skin, black eyes, and most importantly, the stack of thick, black hair, just like Michelle's, made me crazy! I stood there, frozen, and didn't know what to say. Hilo glanced at me, then said something to Mona in his language. She replied boldly, smiled at me, and went into a group of young people who were drinking something from tall, thin glasses.

Hilo put a hand on my shoulder and uttered with a smile, 'Brother, I need to speak to you about Mona. I know what happened between you and Johnny in the restaurant. He's not mad anymore, you didn't know each other, and you were not the first to start a fight. You had a right to defend yourself; this is a normal confrontation between men. You are clean here. I see you like my sister and this is also normal, she can make any guy crazy, but the problem is that Johnny is terribly in love with her, get it? So, forget about her, I'll find you a new girl as good as Mona; we have a lot of them here.'

I burst out laughing and jokingly remarked that really, I liked his sister, but I was not intending to crush someone's happiness.

Hilo became cheerful. We had a drink, talked about this and that, and then he asked me if I had reached a decision.

'You know, Hilo,' I answered, 'thank you very much for your generous proposal to become your partner, but this isn't a business for me. I don't know anything about it, and I don't want to be in somebody's lap, so let's just be friends.'

Hilo smiled and with relief, said, 'I understood what you're saying, but there's only one thing I don't agree with: we're brothers, not friends! Brothers 'til the end of our days, ok?'

With gratitude, I nodded in agreement.

'Now about the money, give me a little time to collect the box and I will pay you as promised. Everything will be divided fairly, just like in a bank,' he chuckled.

'Hilo, brother, thank you for being the same as you always were. I don't need anything extra, I'll be happy with whatever you give me and that will be fair enough. You don't need to be in a hurry with giving me my fair portion. I like it here in your motherland, and if you don't mind, I'll stay in Hawaii. So, help me out if you can to open up a legitimate business.'

'Legit, illegit, no problem. What do you want to start with?'

Suddenly I recalled how Mark had gotten really upset right after one of his meetings and told me that the sugar business was dead.

'We need to get invested into restaurants and hotels. Tourism is the future of these islands,' Mark said. So, I decided to go into hospitality.

We agreed on the following: Hilo would hire me to work in one of his hotels, I would learn the business from the ground up, and then if I like it, he would help me to buy my own small hotel. It appeared that Hilo was from a well-off family. His father had owned two hotels, both of which offered a modest but stable income. Hilo had finished college and good prospects opened up to him, but he was adventurous by nature. One day when his father decided to marry him off to his friend's daughter, he ran away to America. His father disowned him and gave all the inheritance to his daughter, Mona.

As I mentioned, Hilo went through the school of hard knocks in the slums of New York and was on the edge of desperation when fate brought us together. The only thing he wanted at that time was to earn some money to get back home. The years of absence from his native land forced upon him a love of the paradise in this corner of the world.

Hilo returned with our money after his father died. He started to spin around in the shady drugs business and got rich. In order to launder the money, he bought some hotels on the island, including two small ones from Mona. Hilo paid her more money than they were really worth, for Mona to be able to buy a stylish hotel in a prestigious area. So, Hilo decided to send me to her hotel for 'the good of the young ingénue' new to the hospitality industry.

Needless to say, I was ecstatic with this plan but tried not to show my happiness. Hilo called Mona, and they talked for a long time in Hawaiian. I saw Mona turn to look at me and smiled. Hilo came up to me while Mona went back to her friends, but this time, without glancing at me.

'Well, brother, everything is all set, Mona is a hospitality expert. You'll work a little bit at her place, and when you're ready, we'll buy you a nice hotel that will allow you to live without worrying about money,' he said, rubbing his hands.

'I have only one request. Forget that Mona is a woman. It's obvious that she likes you, but for God's sake, don't even think about doing anything that would offend Johnny. Mona is smart, but you know how women don't go by logic but by emotions. I hope you understood me, brother.'

'Yeah, I got it,' I answered without hesitation.

At that moment, I really believed my own words, but I didn't know that "Madame Love," for which no boundaries exist, had already firmly nestled herself in my heart...

In our first meeting, I told Mona about my promise to Hilo, and we agreed there would only be a business relationship between us.

Days flew by. I immersed myself in the job, trying to learn everything I could. I saw Mona briefly every day, trying not to talk to her about anything but work. Johnny would come to pick her up each evening in his fancy car, and they would go out to eat somewhere or to party with their large group of friends. Sometimes they invited me, but I would always say I was busy. I knew that Mona didn't love Johnny and was bored with him. I also knew that she had fond feelings toward me. It was hard to restrain myself. I tried not to look into her big, black eyes, but it was becoming more and more difficult not to...

The managing of the hotel was a demanding but simple business. I had been a very good student and it was time to call Hilo to do our next step in the business plan – to buy a hotel for me - but I was procrastinating. Sadly, I had to acknowledge that I would no longer have the opportunity to see Mona every day. I knew she was thinking about that, too.

On one such day, we stayed in her office until dusk. Mona, to my surprise, was not in a hurry, and Johnny was nowhere to be found. It was really hot. We looked through some bills, and with sleepiness, I leaned back in my armchair.

'Well, you did a good job, really a good job!' Mona complimented with a smile.

'Thank you, Mona. I think you taught me everything that I needed, and I can call tomorrow to Hilo that the 'young ingénue' is ready,' I said with sadness.

Mona looked down and quietly murmured, 'They flew to Los Angeles today for a week. So, you have a little time to rest.'

'And who are they?'

'Hilo and Johnny,' she answered quickly, and then with a sound of irritation, threw out, 'Now run away from here since you've already learned everything.'

Suddenly it struck me as funny. 'You're kicking me out, Madame?' I asked, laughing. 'Don't I deserve a better farewell party?'

She smiled and asked warmly, 'What do you want, my dear cousin?'

'Well, my dear cousin, at least let's go somewhere and celebrate the accomplishment of my work in your company,' I answered quickly, getting up.

She smiled warily. 'It's not a bad idea, George, but I'm too tired to go anywhere. If you don't mind, let's just have a drink here and listen to some music.'

I happily agreed. Mona called out some orders, and soon, the table was set on the balcony.

A full moon was shining, and a gentle breeze was blowing in from the sea. We were drinking wine and talking. I don't recall what we discussed, probably something unimportant, but our eyes talked about something different. You cannot hide the kind of love that like an avalanche crashes through every dam. That kind of love will force you to betray, to sell-out, to forget about everything and everyone! And indeed, we did forget about everything: about Johnny, about Hilo, about traditions and promises. We stood kissing each other on the balcony while the moon condemned us and goggled at us its yellow Hawaiian snout.

'I love you!' was the only phrase we were able to utter…

Six days belonged to us. And what great six days! We were obsessed with each other, swimming in happiness, drunk on love, and couldn't get enough.

The night before Johnny and Hilo's arrival, Mona cried. In the early morning, when she had already opened up the door to leave, she suddenly turned her face to me, and blowing a kiss, merrily shouted, "I love you, I love you more than life itself!" and ringing out with laughter, ran away.

The next day, I came to her hotel to pick up some documents and to call Hilo, so that we could get together. Mona wasn't there, and jealousy put a thorn in my heart. What is she doing now? Is she talking with that zit? Or is she trying to salve her guilt by flirting with him?

The concierge interrupted my thoughts by telling that someone was calling me to the phone. It was Mona. She could barely hold back her tears and revealed that she had told Johnny everything about us!

'George, I'm so sorry, but I can't tolerate him anymore. I love you and only you. I spit on all of these silly prejudices and archaic traditions!'

Everything inside me froze. It wasn't Johnny that scared me but Hilo! How could I ever look in his eyes again after breaking the promises I had made to him? What would he say and think about me?

But pure love was weeping in the phone, a pure, first-time-in-love soul was weeping!

Oh, well, I thought. Seven problems, one answer, and firmly uttered into the phone, 'Mona, my darling, calm down, I'm here with you. You didn't do anything wrong.'

"George, my love, I'm not afraid for myself, they're not going to do anything to me. I'm afraid for you!' she interrupted me.

I tried everything to calm her down, telling her that Hilo would understand, promising to come over right now and talk to him, but the moment I hung up, another call came in and the concierge handed me the phone again – it was Hilo.

'George, you have to come over right away. I have to speak to you as soon as possible,' he threw it like an order and hung up. I detected the strong anger and irritation in his voice.

Within ten minutes, I barged into his office. Johnny was there.

As if nothing had happened, I greeted Hilo. He nodded his head, but Johnny didn't even look at me. He was pale. Hilo looked like he was full of rage. He talked a lot and made all kinds of accusations about my ingratitude. He talked about the traditions of his people and accused me of stomping all over them. Then I got mad.

'You know, Hilo,' I said resolutely, 'I didn't insult or stomp on your culture, I respect this land and your people, and I have always deferred to your traditions, but love is love! I can't order my heart not to love Mona and neither can she force herself to marry a guy she can't stand! You yourself told me how your father wanted to marry you off to a woman you didn't love. Even you rebelled and ran away from here! Why? Because to live with someone you don't love is a prison. Now you want your own sister to marry a man she doesn't love? Why?'

'You don't understand, George!' Hilo shouted, 'this is not your fucking America and not your Russia! Here, we have different customs nobody can mess with, especially when the honor of a man is offended. His honor! You offended him!' Hilo pointed to Johnny, who with a burning hatred, stared at me. 'We cannot forgive such a thing. This is the law of the land on which you are standing right now! Do you get it?'

'Yes, I've got it,' I said humbly. 'I'm ready to accept the consequences, if that's what I must do according to your laws. If you want to kill me, go ahead and kill me, maybe it will be better because I cannot stop loving Mona...'

Hilo looked at me with surprise. It seemed like he was expecting something else. He was quiet for a while, then asked Johnny something in Hawaiian. Johnny was explaining and gesticulating wildly for a long time, then suddenly got up and left.

Hilo rubbed the back of his head in thought, invited me to sit down, and took out a bottle of whiskey. We drank and Hilo, without looking into my eyes, announced, 'Johnny has a right to his revenge...sorry, brother, but you did this to yourself and I warned you...'

'Hilo, you know I'm not afraid to die and won't even resist. If I'm guilty, I'm guilty. Do whatever you're supposed to do in this case,' I answered decisively.

Hilo looked at me again like he was just seeing me for the first time, 'George, I know that you're a fair guy. If I could only save you, I would give up my own life without even blinking, but in this particular situation, I can't do anything. I refuse to betray the rules I've defended all my life. Thank you for not trying to save your own skin as others might do in your place. And thank you that you did not blacken Mona's name by denying your feelings toward her. She is the only person in the world for whom I would live once...once you're not here anymore,' his voice suddenly lowered.

He got up, went to the window, and staring out slowly continued, 'Johnny is a man of honor, so even if he kills you, that still won't restore his authority in the eyes of our people. He wants to prove that even if you're stronger than him, he isn't afraid of you. That's why he is choosing a kind of competition that will give you both a 50/50 chance. He has chosen a game of *Russian Roulette* but on the condition that you spin the barrel in front of Mona.'

I stiffened. I was ready for anything but not this!

I turned to Hilo and tried to convince him to change the conditions, proposing anything, including committing suicide in front of his people. I begged Hilo to be merciful to Mona and not to involve her in this, but he refused to change anything…

What could I do? I had to take part in this barbaric duel that my forefathers had introduced to the world…

The 'duel' was to take place immediately. Hilo called someone, gave instructions, and then we went to his villa. Passing by the hotel, I asked him if I could go up to the room to write a farewell note and to pray. He didn't object. I went up to my room and prayed to the icon that Father Mikhail had once given me, asking the Lord to forgive my worldly sins. Then I wrote a brief letter, where in the case of my death, Hilo was to give all my money to that small Russian church where I had carried the bricks. I put the envelope into my pocket, exited, and we rode…"

The old man turned silent, then he slowly lit a new cigar and looked at me.

"What happened then?" I asked impatiently. His story had me so involved that I got irritated when he stopped.

"What happened then? I don't like to remember that day. You wouldn't believe it, Pasha, but in old age, I have become so sentimental. Sometimes when I don't sleep, I play back my whole life in my head, and maybe it's strange, but I blame myself for a lot of things. On that day, I acted badly. I shouldn't have accepted the duel, it was against God's will, and God doesn't forgive those kinds of things…

Briefly speaking, we went to Hilo's villa, downstairs to a room in his basement that was simply furnished but cozy. There was already a group of unfamiliar Hawaiians sitting in big armchairs, drinking whiskey with ice. Hilo greeted them loudly. They turned to us, answered his greeting, and looked at me. It wasn't hatred in their eyes but rather a gloomy indifference.

Pretty soon, here came Johnny, and Hilo started talking to him. It was quiet, but my heart was pounding just like it always does before a fight in the ring. Suddenly, a door opened and Mona entered, followed by a couple of guys. Her face was pale and her brows were creased. She didn't make eye contact with anyone. It was obvious that she had been brought there against her will.

Hilo got up and addressed everyone:

'Gentlemen, you are here at the request of our brother, Johnny. He is my friend and a brother to me since childhood. You all know how much I love him, and I have proved it many times. There's no need to remind of the times Johnny and I saved each other's lives. You also know about George, whom I've told you about many times. You also know that I'm indebted to him. Without his heroic actions in New York, I would not be here now. In fact, your lives would have turned out very different, and I'm pretty sure your lives couldn't be any better than they are now. You all know that he is my true brother.

So, between these two brothers, there has been a misunderstanding. Of course, this sometimes happens in families. And like any proper family, we have to resolve this. George has not denied his guilt and he hasn't asked for mercy, but on the contrary, he is ready to atone himself with his own blood. During a recent conversation with me, he even asked about the possibility to commit suicide right in front of your eyes!

According to our customs, Johnny has the right to retaliation. His wish must be fulfilled without any question. He has the right to kill the offender, to cut his throat, to drown him, in other words, basically to do whatever he wants to do with him. But our brother Johnny didn't want to do that. He is a man of honor and he doesn't want reprisals but a fair duel. And for the duel, he has chosen *Russian roulette* as a compliment to his Russian brother George. The winner takes all: life and …Mona.

'Hilo, stop it! This is savagery!' Mona jumped up, then turned to Johnny, 'Johnny, I love you, you know that – I love you like a brother, like a brother, do you understand!? Please, don't be angry at me or George. Forgive us! We didn't mean to offend you, we simply love each other. It's nobody's fault! You should at least understand that I will never be yours! I would rather die!"

Johnny jumped up, his eyes were glistening with anger. He uttered something in Hawaiian, but getting himself together, he slowly but firmly uttered in English,

'Thank you, Mona, for calling me a brother, but I love you more than a sister. I have loved you my entire life, and as it was said here correctly, you cannot command the heart and I won't hand you over to anybody – you'll be mine! I don't blame you, you are only a woman. The one to blame is him! These Gringos think the whole world belongs to them. They think they can come into a foreign land and do whatever they want and kidnap our girls, but this Gringo has miscalculated. Nobody can insult me in front of my brothers. Nobody!'

Johnny was unstoppable. His eyes were lightening. His hands were flailing all around in the air, and he was frothing at the mouth.

He turned to me with hatred, like he wanted to kill me with each word he was pronouncing: 'You and I are mortal enemies. There isn't room for both of us on this earth. One of us will die here today, and let God himself choose who will stay and who will go – who will go to heaven and who will go to hell!'

Mona got paler and turned to leave. Hilo tried to stop her, but she looked at him with her black eyes in such a way that he had to step aside.

Before exiting, she suddenly turned to me and shouted, 'George, whatever happens, remember, I love only you and I will be yours or nobody's,' and she slammed the door.

Johnny wanted to go after her, but Hilo stopped him. Everyone focused on me.

I stood up assuredly and said that I was ready for the duel. Hilo took out a revolver, put in a bullet, spun the barrel, and tossed a coin. I was unlucky. I had the first shot. I whispered a prayer to myself, cocked the gun, and put it to my temple, said,

'Whatever we're doing here is a crazy and stupid crime before Mona and love! But I see you're hell-bent on doing it, and I can't stop you and don't have the right to refuse. My dear brother Hilo, I have offended you, I undermined you in the eyes of your friends. Forgive me if you can!'

Hilo got pale and his eyes teared up.

'And to you, Johnny, I say you called me an ungrateful Gringo. This is not true! I never offended you or your country in any way. When I gave Hilo the money in New York, I wasn't an unthankful Gringo. I wasn't an unthankful Gringo when the cops were busting up my ribs trying to find out where Hilo was. You may ask why after acting like that am I not shrinking away from Mona? The answer is simple - because love has always been the condition of human beings. Because it is given to us by God! It isn't my fault that Mona chose me, not you. I tried to do everything, so this ridiculous *Roulette* would not take place, but I know you're bloodthirsty, and one way or another, you're going to pursue it. So, let it be, but ultimately, you'll be the loser. Mona will never be yours!'

People sitting next to our *Roulette* table got quiet. Hilo was staring down, only Johnny was peering at me with malicious pleasure.

I said everything I needed to say, and closing my eyes, I pulled the trigger. The trigger clicked dryly without a shot!

I heard someone shriek with disappointment. I was standing there paralyzed without comprehension...

Since then I have replayed this moment in my mind many times, trying to recall what happened after I pulled the trigger but couldn't remember. It's impossible to describe that moment! I think it was easier to die than to actually survive it – I had made peace with the eventuality of death – and in a way, it was harder to return to the world again.

So, I was still standing there with my eyes closed, afraid to open them. My legs were shaking, and my mouth was dry. Hilo walked over to me and unclamped my hands from the revolver. I opened my eyes and collapsed onto the chair.

Hilo spun the barrel again, gave the gun to Johnny, and patted his shoulder. Voices cheered him on. Johnny carelessly raised his hand to calm his friends down.

"You know, George," he said my name for the first time ever, "it's only now that I have come to understand that you're an honorable man, not an ignorant Gringo who's just hanging out on our beaches. But you have made a mistake in one thing. You don't know our women. Mona is too young; she's just a child who doesn't know what she wants. The kind of love you always talk about will disappear after the first wedding night. Believe me, Mona will be mine, I know my destiny...'

I saw Hilo furl his brow and understood that Johnny's words hurt him.

Johnny poured a full glass of whisky, raised it, and with a false bravado, nodded to his friends, gulping it down. Then he put the revolver to his temple, yelled something in Hawaiian, and pulled the trigger. There was a terrible blast, and Johnny fell down dead!

Smoke, screams, and the sound of the falling chairs...everyone ran to Johnny. Hilo was very pale. He took me by the hand and we left the room. Right away we got to his study. He said something to me and went out, locking the door behind him. I sat down on the chair, exhausted, and waited for him. He returned back in a while, calm, with a bottle of whiskey. We talked through the night, but everything was foggy for me. I got completely drunk, and I couldn't remember how I got back to my hotel.

The next morning, I was awoken by a knock at the door. I opened it, and Mona was standing there. She was ecstatic! We merged into one - her tears, her stormy caress, her young dark-skinned body - everything intertwined to carry us off on the breeze into a land of happiness. And that day lasted long...

After some time, we were quietly married, inviting only Hilo and a few of Mona's friends. We didn't need anybody; we were burning with love, we loved!

The day after the ceremony, Hilo showed up right away and gave us two tickets for a round-the-world cruise. It was the kind of gift we could only have dreamed about. We were beyond happiness! But when we found out that the ship was leaving the same day later that evening, we felt that something was wrong. Hilo was a little jumpy and evaded all of our questions, joking around, saying that he bought the tickets a long time ago but had wanted to make it a surprise for us. Of course, we didn't believe him. Then he carelessly said that there were some problems but not to be worried. 'Just leave right now. When you come back, everything will be fine.'

He saw us off the same night. I'll never forget our farewell when he hugged me so strongly and whispered into my ear, 'Take care of her!' and his voice cracked.

As our ship was leaving, he stood on the pier surrounded by his bodyguards, smoking and from time to time waving to us.

Love, as we know, is selfish. We stood on the deck for a little while and felt sad. But when the city had disappeared behind the waves, we kissed each other and forgot about everything else in the world.

I don't remember how many countries we visited together then. The communications of today didn't exist back then, and we didn't want to get in touch with anyone. It suited me just fine and Mona, too, in the beginning. But soon I started to notice that my "little native," as I called her with love, began feeling sad. I knew she was homesick.

A couple of times I noticed that she was crying, and I tried to comfort her, which sometimes helped, but she was upset more and more frequently. It was time to get back home to Hawaii. When I told her about it, she cheered up, and like a happy child, started packing her things right away. We got off the ship in Canada without finishing our cruise and flew back to Los Angeles straight away. I wanted to stay a little longer in the City of Angels, but Mona insisted on buying tickets for the very next day.

As we approached Honolulu, Mona pressed herself up against me and sobbed. I started to comfort her by telling that everything would be fine and that we're almost home.

'No, my love, nothing is OK! Something has happened to Hilo, something terrible!' she uttered through her tears.

'Come on! That's crazy. Where did you get that from?' I smiled.

'I can't explain how I know, George, sweetheart,' she whispered and leaned against me. I gently caressed her cheek and said nothing, writing off her words to feminine sentimentality.

But Mona was correct in her premonition. Her sensitive heart somehow mystically guessed that something sorrowful had taken place. One week before our arrival, exactly the same night that Mona started to cry and I had decided to return to Hawaii, Hilo was murdered by one of Johnny's relatives.

I cannot express what we felt when we heard the news.

Our tears were not dried up yet when the police descended on us. One of Hilo's "friends" had informed them about the money from the New York robbery and about some underground narcotics ring. Mona and I were arrested. Hilo's property was confiscated, and dozens of his business partners were thrown into jail. But soon after an investigation, they liberated me and Mona without finding any evidence of our criminality: I had already served my time for the New York robbery, Mona's money wasn't connected with Hilo's underground business, and I had not yet received anything from him."

My mobile phone suddenly rang. My wife was back from her excursion and said that she would meet me at the beach in 15 minutes. Figuring out from my brief conversation that I had to go, the old man stood up.

"Aren't you tired of my fairy tales yet?" he asked smiling.

"No, not at all!" I exclaimed. "Thank you so much for everything, for your hospitality, and especially for your story! But I can't leave without knowing how it all ends! Yegor Pavlovitch, quickly tell me what happened with you and Mona!"

The old man smiled the kind of smile only happy people have.

"Well, Pasha, there's nothing to tell. Mona and I lived in bliss and harmony for many years. And would you believe, my friend, that every day I still thank the Lord for every moment of our life together. She was a saintly woman! Throughout my long life, I have seen how other people live fighting, cursing, hating, and betraying each other. It's miserable to see how men are like women now and women act like men, crude, harsh, and without charm. Mona was different, she was a real woman. Well, it's impossible to tell everything about her...

She died suddenly from cancer. My son and I were left alone. He was a late-in-life child for us. For a long time, the Lord did not bless us with children. I always thought that was the price I had to pay for my sins. I prayed day and night, asking for a miracle, and at last, He performed a miracle. He gave us a son and then took Mona away. We should be careful what we pray for, especially when asking for miracles. I believe God doesn't like that. Whatever fate hands to you, you should accept it gratefully. A miracle is not an earthly concept. We are born to suffering and loss. The Lord tests us here, but we will live up there," the old man said, pointing to the sky. "Now I have only one true happiness – my son. I'll raise him and then I will fly away to my loved ones, to Michelle, to Mona…"

I was simply stunned how casually he uttered one last phrase about God, life, and death. Something gentle and sad touched my heart. I didn't want to leave this complex old man with his vulnerable, difficult, but beautiful fate. I felt like a person who had just finished watching a tremendous movie that had absorbed his imagination so much that he didn't want to leave the theatre and was sitting and watching the credits, trying for a moment to prolong the story which had kept his attention the whole performance…

But it was time to leave, so we got up and went to the exit. Passing by the room that I had first thought was an office, I saw a huge portrait of an unusually beautiful woman and unwittingly stopped before it.

"That is my Mona!" I heard the quiet voice of the old man behind my back.

"What a beautiful woman!" I said aloud.

"Her insides were even a hundred times more beautiful than her outsides," the old man smiled sadly, then remembering something, he suddenly asked, "Are you going to visit our Motherland, I mean Uralsk?"

"Probably this summer if all goes as planned. Do you have any special requests?"

The old man vacillated, reflecting on something and finally said, "You're the first and for sure the last compatriot whom I will meet here at the end of the world. For me, today's meeting with you was like a confession to the Motherland. She did not always treat me with love, but as I said, you cannot stay angry with her. We were born to that country and not to any other. Through all these years, I have never forgotten who or what I am. I am, was, and will always be a Russian Cossack and I'm proud of it. So, brother, I have one request, if you're willing to accept great, if not, I'll understand and won't be upset. When you're in Uralsk, would you be able to collect a handful of soil from *Kureni* and send it to me here? I will pay for all your expenses." The old man reached for his wallet, but I stopped him.

"Yegor Pavlovitch, give me your address, and by all means, I'll do whatever I can. Don't think twice about it, and don't offend me by offering the money."

"Well, thank you, my brother!" he said happily. "I would like to have it, so that when my time comes, I'll have a handful of native earth with me," tears were shining in his eyes. He stretched his hand out with a business card.

We left the office. It was a velvety warm evening. The beautiful palms were propping up with their slender trunks, the purple sky sketched into the January evening. A light breeze blew in from the sea. I felt warm and sentimental as I said goodbye forever to someone now so close to me, practically a relative! The old man's strong, pure, and unusual story had made me anxious.

When we hugged each other, I could feel his surprisingly strong shoulders trembling. He was a little embarrassed by his tears and gently pushed me away, turned around, and disappeared behind the doors of his office. I saw my wife standing alone at the appointed place under a palm and walked toward her.

A few years passed before I was able fulfill the old man's request. During all that time, I was sending him Christmas cards and receiving back little notes in which the old man was telling me that everything was fine. I felt a little guilty but couldn't escape the everyday routine of life in order to get back to my homeland. The old man pretended to forget his request and didn't remind me about it.

At last, I slipped out of my comfortable and busy American life and journeyed to my native Uralsk. The city had changed so much, it was almost unrecognizable. Only the Ural River was the same, its strong current flowing southward, and the powerful Uralsk winds blew the same with the bittersweet smell of the steppes wormwood.

After taking care of paperwork formalities, visiting the graves of my friends and family, fishing on the small river Derkul, and reliving childhood dreams, I began a search for the relatives and friends of Yegor Pavlovitch. But all of my attempts to find someone who had ever known him or his family were in vain. In place of his childhood home now stood an apartment block. There were few Russians still left in the city. The new sovereign state of Kazakhstan had gobbled up this luxurious piece of land that had fallen into its lap from drunk Yeltsin's shoulders.

I did not have anyone to turn to that knew Yegor Pavlovitch. I tried to find the old documents of his family. I went to the city hall where they didn't want to speak to me in Russian and then it got even worse. When they found out I was a U.S. citizen, they refused to give me any information because I was a "foreigner."

I left the city feeling that I had forever lost my homeland. The Ural River looked with condemnation, as if I was guilty for what had happened to her land...

A day before my departure, I came to the church to pray. On the steps of the old Cossack cathedral, an ancient man was sitting and begging for money. I gave him some small change and asked to pray for Yegor Pavlovitch Lebedikhin.

"Which Lebedikhin?" he asked with his toothless mouth and stared at me with faded burned-out eyes.

I told him about the Russian Hawaiian who had once called this city home.

"You mean Gorka? The one who went missing in action? It can't be!" the grandpa exclaimed.

I slumped down near him, my heart was pounding. We started to talk. His name was Martimyan.

"Did I know Gorka?" the old man repeated. "Not only did I know him, but he was like a brother to me! We used to hang out together all the time," and moving his toothless mouth, added, "Oh good God, he showed up at Anaii, and I thought he perished in somewhere in Germany!"

I smiled and did my best to explain that his friend hadn't shown up in Anaii but Hawaii! I don't think the old man knew where Hawaii was, but for sure, he understood it was very far away.

"Martimyam, are any of Yegor's relatives alive?" I asked, daring not to hope.

"No, the father was arrested by the NKVD, you know, during the war. Why and for what, I don't know, I won't lie. There was a rumor that it was because Gorka could have run off to the Germans or for something else."

The old man was talking slowly in an old Cossack Uralsk dialect that can't be confused with any other. I listened to each word anxiously.

"Well, his mother died in the '60's. His brother drank himself to death but his nephew Sergeyka is alive."

My heart throbbed with happiness!

"He's alive?!" I asked briskly. "Do you know where he lives?"

"Of course, I do, dear man. He is my *shabra* – a neighbor in your Russian language."

I was in 7th heaven. It wasn't hard to convince the old man to show me Sergey's house. They lived not too far from the church. I followed the old man until we came to a dirty potholed street where he pointed at an old dilapidated house.

"Well, Sergeyka lives right there. Go on over, and I have to return back to my place near the church. Maybe I'll get some money for bread," said the old man and cunningly looked at me. I handed over to him a pretty good sum in local currency. His eyes lit up and quickly, without thanking me, he went around the church to a liquor store at the end of the street.

I knocked on a small window with old shutters. A strong, neatly dressed man of about my age came out. It was Sergey. First, he was suspicious, but when he found out that I was from America, he suddenly softened and invited me inside, taking out a bottle of local vodka and some snacks.

A little bit later, his wife and daughter showed up, and I repeated the story of their relative one more time. Sergey's wife wasn't happy with the news that the old man had been found. But the daughter, on the other hand, eagerly asked about Grandpa Gora, his business, his son, and Hawaii. As for Sergey, he sat quietly and knitted his brow.

The bottle was empty, my curiosity had been satiated, it was time to leave. I reached out to give Yegor Pavlovitch's business card to Sergey, and much to my disappointment, he refused to take it.

"You know, my uncle chose that life himself," he explained with some nervousness. "My grandma, his mother, waited for his return up until her last breath. Her poor heart believed that he was alive, but through all those years, he couldn't even manage to send her a little note! That's why I cannot forgive him!"

I knew that no explanation would satisfy him, so doubting a positive response, I asked, "Well, what should I tell him?"

Sergey shrugged his broad shoulders. "Tell him what I have just said." Then, when we were outside, he held out his large calloused hand, and added, "Or maybe just tell him you couldn't find anyone. It would be better like that for everyone, I guess..."

I noticed that his wife and daughter, Svetlana, were standing silently behind him near the gate. The wife's face was impenetrable, but Svetlana's black teenaged eyes were full of displeasure from her father's words.

I said good-bye and walked along the former *Sovetskaya Street*, now changed by the Kazakh nationalists into *Abai Avenue*, to the city center and tried to catch a taxi.

It was already dark. Heavy dark clouds were rolling toward the weary city. The smell of rain was in the air. I heard somebody's light footsteps behind me. It was Svetlana.

"I'm so sorry!" She puffed, catching her breath.

"For what?" I asked surprised.

"For Papa. He is very rigid and quick to judge!" She looked around and asked, "Could you give me Uncle Gora's business card? I would like to write him a letter."

My soul melted, I handed over the card, and gave her a little parting hug.

Back in the States, I took out a packet full of Uralsk soil and divided it into two parts. One part I put into the wooden lacquer box that I bought in Moscow and hid it in my desk just for myself. The other one, I carefully packed and mailed to my Hawaiian compatriot.

A week later, my home phone rang. A voice spoke in Russian with a light accent. He asked my name. It was Paul, Yegor Pavlovich's son.

"I am calling you to thank for the little bit of earth from my father's Motherland. From your letter, I could tell that you don't know what misfortune has befallen us; Yegor Pavlovich has died. He passed away at the beginning of May very quickly without much warning. Before he died, he told me about your promise to send some Uralsk earth, and he explained to me what to do with it upon his death. I told him that you had probably forgotten about your promise and asked his permission to call and remind you, but my father said that you are a Uralsk Cossack and that the Cossacks always keep their word! Now I see he was right. I'm so sorry for not giving you the benefit of the doubt. Thank you for remembering my father. I have already visited him at the cemetery and poured the Uralsk soil onto the grave just as he would have wanted. Last night, I dreamt that Papa was smiling."

Tears came to my eyes. I told him something chaotically about my trip to Uralsk, about Svetlana, and his relatives there. Paul detected my mood.

"Thank you for everything. I've read your letter to my dad, and I am waiting impatiently for news from Sveta."

I couldn't fall asleep that night. It was stuffy. I got up and went downstairs, opened the fridge and took out the bottle of *Stoli*, poured a glass full, and went out into the backyard.

The night smelled of rain, and I could hear the rolling thunder. I looked at the black, forbidding sky and whispered, *"God's kingdom to you, Cossack!"*[5] and threw back the vodka that was bitter, like man's fate.

Then I sat down on the cool lawn and looked up at the sky again. Something solemn and powerful was there - something that made me, the trees, the houses, the cars parked in the street, even the whole planet seem small and insignificant. It began to drizzle. First, bigger drops pricked at my face, then the rain-drops grew and grew until finally the clouds burst open. I sat motionless on the grass. The rain streamed down my cheeks, shoulders, and body. I was soaked through and got up. Suddenly I tasted salt on my lips. It was tears – those rare, repressed,

---

[5] The religious wish to a deceased person. (Rus.).

masculine tears that had not fallen for a long time! A weight was lifted from my soul, which became lighter and calmer.

I smiled and went back inside.

Hawaii - Uralsk - Colorado Springs

Sharik

To my childhood dog

Recently while sorting through some old books in my basement, I came across a small volume of poems authored by a long forgotten but wonderful poet, *Eduard Asadov*. He lost his eye sight in the war and was little known to a wide circle of readers, but his simple and somewhat naive poems were imbued with such thrilling romanticism that took hold of one's memory forever.

My heart started beating both quickly and merrily at once. For some reason, I recalled the lines from his poem about a ginger color mutt that the owner deserted at the train station because it was not of "noble blood." The train moved forward with the mutt's cruel owner on board, but the poor dog ran and ran until he stumbled onto the railings of the bridge and died. The poem finished with these words forever seared into my memory:

> *... The old man, you don't know the Nature,*
> *It can be the body of a mutt,*
> *But the heart could be of a purest breed!*

A mutt with a heart like that of a purebred. What boy from my generation of children, having grown up among the hungry post-war villages of the former Soviet Union, did not own such a dog?

I, too, owned such a childhood mutt. His name was Sharik. My father had picked up this puppy somewhere off the street and brought it home in his cap. It was brownish-red, and at the beginning when my father stepped into our yard, we thought that he was carrying a loaf of rye bread. We lived very poorly, like all Soviet people after World War II. My father and mother worked in a small factory. My grandmother, Babaka, as the Cossacks called their babushkas, looked both after us and our simple household, consisting of a cow named *Malinka**, six geese, and a dozen chickens. By "after us," I mean after me, my two twin brothers, *Tolka* and *Kolka*, two years older than me, and the youngest, *Petka*[6].

When we found out that our father had brought home a puppy, our happiness was unlimited! The dog was so funny that he overtook our hearts immediately. Only one person in our family, however, was not happy - Babaka.

"Why in the world, Gregory, have you brought an extra mouth home to our family? How will I feed him? We could soon turn up our own toes!" she grumbled. Her voice held no rigor, and a little grumbling was in her character.

The arguments on what to call the puppy had commenced. Many variants emerged: Doggy, Cur, Tuzik, Lump. The twins almost got into a fight. Only Babaka, who did not take part in the dispute, remained silent.

We sat down to supper. The dog was placed on a bench next to the stove. He was so small, a red lump with no tail. We had finished our dinner, and suddenly, someone knocked over the bench, sending our

---

[6] **Malinka* – Rasberry (diminutive form). **Tolka, Kolka, Petka* – nick names for Anatoli, Nikolai, Pyotr.

puppy rolling like a ball to the door. All stood still as Babaka exclaimed, *"A taint will take you!"**, just as *sharik***[7] started rolling!

Our father smiled, "Well, here is a proper name for this dog: Sharik." Everyone laughed, and no one objected to this suggestion.

The days passed quickly. We were growing up, and Sharik was growing up, too. Only he was growing very slowly, and soon, stopped growing altogether.

To our father's great displeasure, Sharik turned out to be a simple mutt, a small, kind, and affectionate mutt.

"Well, what kind of dog is this that he doesn't bark, and no one is afraid of him? Only wastes bread, just a useless creature!" our father grumbled angrily.

We didn't pay attention to these complaints. Sharik had become our loyal friend, a part of our childhood.

Our father, Gregory, was a good man. He returned home from the war badly wounded; one leg was shorter than the other by a matchbook. There were fragments of a German mine embedded in it.

One spring day, his leg became inflamed. The village boasted no hospital. There was only the local doctor, Aunt Lisa. She examined his leg and noted that the mine's fragments were the problem before saying, "You must go to town for the surgery."

But our father did not go anywhere. He had to earn money for a large family of four children and our mother, who was pregnant with a fifth. He was also the personal driver of the factory owner, Director Kireyev, who was a strict man and did not like when he was asked for favors. He was driving a new car named *"Pobeda."*[8] Of course, our father was afraid to lose his job, and he held on to it tightly.

But his leg remained a source of terrible pain. At night, our father could not sleep. He moaned but did not complain. Only once,

---

[7] *A taint will take you!* – A phrase used to express irritation or a surprise. *Sharik – a small ball.*

[8] *Pobeda* - Victory.

I heard him painfully gasp, "It would be easier to die than to carry this pain!"

"Don't say that!" our mother clasped her hands. She then anxiously asked, "Should I call Lisa?"

"What would your Lisa do?" Babaka asked, angry.

"What do you mean 'What would she do'?" She can give him a pill or something else. She is the doctor after all!" replied Mother.

"Doctor, doctor!" Babaka mocked. "They do not know anything nowadays. Doctors! They are good only to treat horses but not people!" Babaka never visited any doctors and did not believe in them.

"We should pray, and everything will be okay. The Lord is omnipotent. He will heal!"

My mother looked at Babaka with resentment but said nothing. They were at odds with each other, but in front of Father, they never cursed.

Babaka prayed to her time-darkened icons and then she left the house. After some time, she returned with a bucket of fine river sand. Then she got out some rough, old material and crafted an oblong bag from it. She poured in the sand and placed it in the oven to heat up. When the sand became hot, Babaka took out the bag from the oven and wrapped Father's sore leg.

Father stood up, moaning as the sand mercilessly burned his leg. My mother wore a scowl on his face, and Babaka prayed.

In the morning, our father struggled to rise, but he went to work. At night, Babaka continued to pray and place hot sand on his leg. Two days later, Father felt some improvement. Mother continued to change the blood-soaked bandages as the mine's fragments were being drawn out. He soon recovered completely. Babaka claimed triumph, and Mother calmed down.

The summer was miserable, and not a single raindrop fell. A drought lingered. Bread was lacking in the stores. I remember the long lines, standing at the door of the shop, desperately looking down the dusty road winding from the city to our village and us boys, tired of running around, sat in the shade of an old broken horse cart. We were hungry and thirsty, but it was impossible to leave, as the bread was sold only per person to those who waited in line.

A baker usually drove an old, scary "*polutorka*," a small, terribly rattled lorry. Some women from the line helped to unload the loaves of bread. They were allowed to cut to the beginning of the line when they finished unloading. We avidly looked at the rosy, still hot "bricks." I will never forget the smell of that bread.

In late July, the rate of bread, sold to one person was reduced. The quality of the bread had deteriorated. Something had been added. Something that made the bread smell unlike bread.

The rumor was that they had added sawdust to the flour, but people were afraid to say it out loud. The fear of Stalin gripped the hearts of many.

One day, a baker brought greenish, wet bread. Babaka burst into tears. I heard her as she whispered, "We won't get through this winter!" and went to the icons to pray.

Dad came home from his job, grim and weary.

Babaka exclaimed in a fit of rage, "You had better shoot the dog, Grisha, as I have nothing to feed him. The bread that we get from the store is not enough, even for us."

My brothers and I started to cry. Father looked at us and said, "Don't worry, children!" (He always called us children.) I will not kill him, but we cannot keep Sharik with us anymore; he will die of hunger. Tomorrow, the Director is sending me to Kaztalovka, a village far from Uralsk. I will leave Sharik there. The village is large and is actually a district center, so someone will adopt him for sure."

Our father's word in such situations was like law in our family. We understood it and never challenged him. So, we went to bed with tears in our eyes.

The next day, Father took Sharik and left him 100 kilometers from our our village. Dad returned home, sullen and angry. We cried quietly, arguing about Sharik.

Some days passed. The sun scorched both us and the earth mercilessly. Not a single raindrop fell. Babaka covered the windows with old newspapers and opened the door, so it became easier to breathe.

Later in the afternoon, when the heat had subsided, we went out into the yard, and laying in the shade of the barn, we spotted our Sharik! We rushed over to him, but he was barely alive. He was emaciated with a torn ear and only his eyes were full of any expression. We were shouting and leaping with great happiness!

The noise brought Babaka outside. We thought she would be mad at us, but without saying a word, she returned into the house and brought out a small piece of bread and some water, placing both before the dog. She went back inside the house, grumbling something under her breath. Our dog rushed toward the water and emptied the whole bowl. We poured him some more and he finished that, too. Strangely, he didn't touch the bread, even though we urged him to eat it.

Babaka came out again, and Sharik trembled, as though he was guilty of something.

"Wow, what a smart creature!" Babaka clasped her hands together in surprise. "He knows that we are short on bread and doesn't want to be a burden." Then, unexpectedly, she said softly, "Eat, if you managed to come. What are we to do with you?"

To our great surprise, Sharik wagged his dirty tail and swallowed the bread in a moment. "God, I never saw such a dog!" Babaka exclaimed.

In an hour or so, Sharik was running around the yard and barking happily.

Our parents returned home in the evening. We didn't know how to tell them about Sharik. We were especially fearful of our father's reaction, and therefore, hid Sharik behind the barn. But our secret was quickly exposed. Mother went to the outhouse and saw the dog. She called our father. To our great delight, Father was not angry.

On the contrary, he exclaimed with odd surprise and happiness, "I cannot believe my eyes! I left him more than a hundred kilometers away! Besides, he was sitting in the trunk and could not see the road. How in the world did he find us?"

It seemed everyone was elated at the dog's return, especially us kids. But the reality of adult responsibility overshadowed the feelings of children, and a little later, Father again took Sharik away, this time even further. It took some time, but yet again, Sharik came back, all tattered and unnaturally thin. This time, Father did not laugh upon seeing the dog and wanted to shoot him with his old hunting rifle. But us kids howled so loudly that our father gave up, "Indulge the children, and let him live for now."

Soon, Khrushchev struck a deal with America and bread became more available. The adults forgot about Sharik for some time.

Summer passed and autumn came, bringing long awaited rains. Snow fell in early November on a wet and happy land. Winter had begun. We spent our days on the street, throwing snowballs, building snow castles, and sledding down hills. Sharik went everywhere with us.

One day, our father left for a long business trip. At night, we heard a noise in the yard. Someone was rolling out a barrel of petrol from our yard! The gasoline was not ours. It belonged to the Director's NZ.[9] Babaka and Mother stood watching from a window because they were afraid to go out.

When Father returned from his trip and learned about the theft, he was terribly angry at all of us. He was angry with Mother and Babaka, who didn't go out of the house. Most of all, he was furious with Sharik.

---

[9] NZ – Russian abbreviation for Emergency Ration.

"What kind of dog is this? Anyone could step on his tail, and he wouldn't even bark! I am going to shoot him!"

In those cruel times, people were shooting old or sick dogs. Therefore, in Father's words, it would not be wild or wrong to shoot Sharik in accordance with the moral laws of the day. But again, our father couldn't bring himself to kill Sharik. Soon, the thief was discovered. He was a chauffeur from the factory, and he himself came and begged for forgiveness from Father. He returned the gasoline, and in a sign of reconciliation, brought a bottle of vodka. The theft had been forgotten, but the fact that someone stole something from our yard, protected by a dog, was like a slap in the face of Father's pride. He could not forgive poor Sharik for this. So, soon, a case emerged to get rid of the "lazy dog."

One day, father took Babaka to visit Uncle Victor, her youngest son. Uncle Victor lived on the state farm, 90 kilometers away from us. Babaka used to go there once a year and usually took one of us along on such trips. This time, the choice fell to me. We arrived at the farm. After exchanging greetings, Aunt Liva, Uncle's Victor wife, invited us to dinner. The adults were sharing bits of news, and Father expressed his frustration with the dog, stating that he didn't know how to get rid of it.

"Bring the dog here," proposed Uncle Victor, sipping tea from the saucer. "There is a strange man, Chernyshov, in our village. He is an accountant. He and his wife live alone with no children. He recently mentioned that he is looking for a good dog. Maybe the mutt would be a good fit for them."

"Good," Father quickly agreed. "In a week or two, I'll return for my mother and Pavlyk and bring the dog."

At these words, Aunt Liva made a wry face. She didn't like her husband's relatives, especially Babaka. She looked at me like I was an ugly duckling, correcting my behavior and preaching at me, telling me what to do and what not to do. I was afraid of her and did not stray far from Babaka, waiting eagerly when Sunday would come and Dad would take us home.

On Saturday, Aunt and Uncle prepared *banya*.[10] Uncle Victor stayed at work late, and the women decided to go to the bath-house first. Babaka wanted me to wait for Uncle Vitya, who would have me washed as my father usually did, but Aunt Liva resisted, "Victor will come home very tired and won't want to deal with him. Besides, he does not like to take care of a child! We will wash him ourselves."

"Liva, I don't think it's a good idea. Don't forget he is a boy and understands everything already," Babaka doubted.

"What can he understand? He is still a milksop," she smiled. Turning to me, she directed, "Off you go!"

The *banya* was very small. It smelled like smoke and was fearfully hot. Babaka wore a long shirt, which covered all of her body except for her arms. There were three washing bowls, which Babaka first filled with hot water and then poured in cold water.

Aunt Liva entered, and seeing that I was in shorts, laughed. "Mother, how come you didn't take of his underwear?" Turning to me, she ordered, "Come on, hero, take off your shorts!" I blushed to the ears but did not dare to disobey.

Aunt Liva quickly slipped out of her dress and became completely naked. She was very beautiful. I had never seen naked women before, and I watched her, spellbound. I knew I should not do this, that it was a shame to stare like this, but I couldn't avert my eyes from her large, white breasts and from the black triangle of hair at the bottom of her abdomen.

"Why are you staring at me?" Aunt Liva rudely shouted. "Come here, I will wash you!"

---

[10] Banya – a bath House.

But I stood, transfixed. Babaka saved the situation. She washed me, dressed me, and sent me out.

The next day, Father came and brought Sharik with him. They tied the dog to a fence and sat down to drink tea. I went to Sharik and started petting him. Sharik wagged his tail. He was so happy to see me, and we began to play.

Soon, Father and Uncle Victor finished their tea, left, and returned with a stout, good-looking man.

"Well, I thought your dog would look like a tiger and here is a simple mutt!" the man smiled.

"Take him, Dmitrich! You won't feel sorry!" replied my father. "The dog looks small, but once chained up, he will be so fearsome that no one would enter your house."

I was really surprised by this advice since we had never chained Sharik. Father was clearly insincere, wishing in any way to get rid of the dog. Dmitrich was a kind man. He laughed, joked, and took our Sharik away.

The winter passed, melting ice filled the brooks, and starlings flew in from the warmer climates. We started to forget about our Sharik. Life had become better, and the famine had retreated.

One day in late April, our father brought home quite a large puppy and as if to soothe his guilt for taking away Sharik from us.

He said, "This is your new dog, your new Sharik. He is a very good breed and will be big and angry."

We first accepted the puppy with some apprehension but emphatically refused to call him Sharik.

Someone called him *Verny*.[11] The puppy grew quickly and soon became a big and very aggressive dog. Our father put him on a chain and was quite proud when, one day, Verny bit a gypsy who tried to steal something from our yard.

---

[11] *Verny* – loyal

Two years passed. It was autumn. Rain fell continuously. On one of these days, while we were sitting at home, the sound of ferocious barking brought us running to the windows. We looked out and saw our Sharik in the yard! Verny and Sharik had entangled themselves together, tearing each other to pieces. We rushed outside to pull them apart.

In the evening, our father came home and tried to banish Sharik from the yard, but the dog wouldn't run far from home. He simply sat down in the shade of the neighbor's wattle fence, looking with anguish toward our yard. Slyly, we snuck over to feed him. A week or so later, Uncle Victor and Dmitrich came. It took them a lot of time and efforts to catch Sharik. Finally, they caught him and put a dog collar on him.

"You know, Grisha," said Dmitrich apologetically, "I haven't seen such an evil dog in my life! I put him on a chain as you advised, and we have since no longer had to lock our house; we sleep now securely. He's a great dog! He understands everything like a human being! Thank you for him!"

"How did he run away from you?" our father asked, sincerely surprised.

"It's beyond me! He has plenty of food, his dog house is spacious, and fresh hay is always available. My wife, Zinaida Ivanovna, adores the dog, treats him like her own child. We thought the dog got used to us and forgot about you and your family. I see now that we were wrong! I let him off the chain for one night in the courtyard, and the dog just disappeared. We discovered him missing in the morning. We searched everywhere in the village and its surroundings but couldn't find him. One of our drivers told me that he saw a dog running along the road in the direction of Uralsk. Well, I understood immediately where he was running to!" sighed Dmitrich. Then he gently patted Sharik and added with obvious admiration, "Wow, a simple mutt possessing such a heart!"

Sharik was taken away once again.

The winter ushered in cold and stinging frosts. In December, Uncle Viktor came to visit his mother and brought with him his usual presents for the New Year: a sack of flour, cream, and some meat with bacon.

Among the news shared around the table, he said, "The Chernyshevs moved into the city."

"And what about Sharik?" asked the twins in unison. "Where is he now?"

Uncle looked at them and grinned, "They took your dog with them to the city. Now he lives on the third floor with them."

"They keep a dog in the house?" Babaka was shocked. At that time, it was unusual for people to have dogs inside the house. At least for people living in the village.

Uncle Viktor snorted. "They are nuts. Not only do they keep your mutt in their flat, they also use their own plates to feed it! They never had children, so that's why Zinaida behaves oddly, washing it in the bathtub, combing it, and walking the dog every morning. Can you imagine?"

We exchanged glances with each other. Tolka frowned. Seeing this, Uncle Victor said, "Your mutt now lives in the lap of luxury. Not even many people live like that. Dmitrich now is a *big bump*.[12] They have more than enough to live on. Now, for sure, your dog will not run away from such a good life; he has certainly forgotten about you!"

"He has not forgotten," Kolka frowned. "You do not know our Sharik!"

Uncle Vitya looked mockingly at him, as he loved to tease us. "Maybe I do not know your mutt as well as you, but I've lived such a large life, milksop, that you could not dream of. God save you from such a life! If I tell you that the dog won't run away from such a good

---

[12] *Big bump* – big cheese – big boss.

life, I mean it! What would he miss here? Hunger, cold, a dirty life?"

"Well, son, about the dirtiness, you are not right," Babaka intervened. "We live like everyone else does, and we are not the worst!"

"I am not referring to the house. I am referring to... generally speaking about life around you." Our father frowned but didn't say anything.

"Well, children, drink your tea and out you go. You shouldn't *hang your ears here.*[13] Let the adults talk!" Mother said. We quickly finished our tea and went to the living room.

Uncle Vitya was respected by the adults in our family. He was Deputy Director of the State farm in the economic sector. Sometimes Father would go to him for help. Uncle always helped but did so with such reluctance that Father asked him only when life was quite unbearable. As children we were afraid and did not like him.

"Uncle is right. Sharik will not come back anymore," Tolka said when we were alone. "No, he will come. You'll see for yourself!" Kolka answered stubbornly. "He loves us!" "You are a fool, Kolka! Didn't you hear what Uncle Victor was saying? They are bathing Sharik in the bathtub, and he eats with them like a human! And you keep repeating this foolishness!" Tolka mimicked him. "He has surely forgotten all about us."

"And what is a bath tap?" I asked timidly.

"Bathtub," Tolka corrected me. "It is a ... big wash basin that city folks have, get it?" I certainly did not understand, but not wanting to appear dense, nodded my head.

"I bet Sharik will come back!" Kolka suddenly exclaimed.

"You want to bet? Ok! What will be your bet?" Tolka got excited. They engrossed themselves in debate. The case had proven to be difficult. They were twins, and our parents always bought them the same

---

[13] *Hang your ears here* – listening openmouthed.

of everything, even toys, so they could offer nothing new to each other. Finally, they bet on *shalbans*.[14] I was appointed as a witness.

That night, Sharik appeared in my dreams. First, he was barking happily and licked my cheek. And then, suddenly, my Uncle Victor materialized and dragged him away. I ran after them and cried.

The winter that year was snowy and frosty. It snowed almost every day, and there was so much snow that we dove into it from top of the sheds head first. Spring came earlier than usual though, and the snow melted fast. Black water flooded all meadows and gullies surrounding the village.

The *Derkul*[15] left the shores, and even though it happened very rarely, flooded homes in the lowlands. There was no bridge between our village and the city at that time. There was only a pontoon crossing, which served as a bridge until the first frosts. Then the pontoons were removed, and the traffic of goods had to be diverted to the city by way of another bridge in the south. People had to cross the river using the railway bridge, built before the 1917 revolution. The traffic resumed when the ice became thicker, and commercial vehicles could cross the river.

On one of those spring days, when the sun sparkled and reflected in millions of puddles, brooks, and puddles, when it rang with happiness awakening after a long hibernation, a dog's frantic barking brought us to the window. We all ran out into the yard and saw Verny was fighting with another dog! How can one describe such an ugly picture: our father disentangling the dogs, both of whom had locked each other in a deadly grasp, and us, jumping and screaming with delight because the other dog was our Sharik!

Sharik was all wet. How had he crossed the *Chagan*[16] that still was

---

[14] *Shalbans* – punishment by hitting the forehead with the fingers.
[15] *The Derkul* – name of the river.
[16] *The Chagan* - river larger in size than the Derkul

full of ice floes? How did he found his way to our village, crossing the unfamiliar streets of the city? These questions were asked by all who became aware of our Sharik's return. Women of the village were surprised, lost in conjectures, and men were teasing our father, heating up his wounded ego.

Our father tried to shoo the dog at first, but this time, we stood up firmly for Sharik. Seeing such resistance, our father gave up.

"What the hell! Let him stay till Dmitrich comes after him. Just tie your dog up in the back yard, so Verny does not to see him."

We did as he instructed, placing Sharik on a chain in the back yard, and Verny chained in the front. They were separated by a small solid fence. All was okay when the gate was closed, but when someone opened it, and they saw each other, both dogs went crazy. Our father was angry.

Spring had passed and summer came. The days rolled by. The Chernyshevs had not arrived. They either had moved somewhere else or finally realized that they could not deter Sharik by any means. It seemed everything was ok then. But life, the greatest dramatist, failed to drop the curtain in that sad story.

For a small household with what little we had, owning two dogs turned out to be expensive and inconvenient. The dogs fiercely hated each other. Our parents came home late from their jobs, and they had not much time until dark to give hay to the cow, clean the shed, give the forage to the chicken and geese, and bring water from the well. And with all that hectic work, they had to also tolerate the "dogs' war!" My parents, wearied by "communist experiments," neither had the time nor the energy to be sentimental. The economic severity of that time weighed heavily upon them. Our father grew increasingly angry, saying that we should do something. All his anger was directed against poor Sharik.

"Well, what's the use of this dog?" he often said. "He neither barks nor bites, only wastes our bread on him!"

These words frightened us kids. We first feared that Father would again give Sharik to someone. But then we calmed down and stopped paying attention to his grumblings. We thought that, in any case, our Sharik would come back home. But we were unfamiliar with the reality of adult life...

One summer day, our father took us to the meadows to mow some hay for our cow, Malinka. We were so happy! The meadows lay on the other side of the Derkul, near the vast factory orchard. The most exciting thing for us was to cross the river by ferry. Dad took the twins and me, leaving our younger brother, Peter, who was only three-years-old, at home with Babaka and Mother. Petka, as we called him, seeing us leaving the yard let out a frantic roar. Babaka distracted his attention, and we went on our way.

On the other side of the river existed a "different world," which fascinated our childish imaginations with whirring of grasshoppers and the croaking of frogs. The birds were twittering, a nightingale launched its trills, but the most fascinating was the screaming of the cuckoo birds! A nursery rhyme inherently learned from childhood asked this question, "Cuckoo, cuckoo, please tell me, how many years have I left to live?"

We were happy when the bird cried many, many times and deeply upset when the bird ceased its cuckooing. We did not know that the mischievous cuckoo knew nothing about how many years each person would walk the earth ...

While our father mowed hay, we ran around, catching butterflies, collecting bugs, and playing hide and seek. It started to get dark. We helped our father fill bags with grass and went back home. Father seemed oddly unsettled. He looked kind of guiltily at us and frowned.

We arrived home when it became completely dark. A dim light shown from the lamp in the kitchen. The smell of fried potato with onion was tantalizing. Tolka went to the outhouse but returned a moment later, confused and saying, "Sharik is not there..."

Kolka and I rushed to the back yard, searched everywhere, but could not find Sharik! His chain lay near the shed in the dust.

Babaka came out on the porch and called us in for supper. We ran to the kitchen, and Father was washing his hands. Mother set the big skillet of fried potato on the table. Petka was sitting by the window and pounded the table with his spoon.

"Wash your hands, children, and sit down to eat," Babaka's voice was indistinct. We washed our hands and sat down at the table. Kolka, the bravest of us, asked, "But, Babaka, where is Sharik?"

Babaka glanced at Father, and looking down quietly replied, "There is no Sharik anymore. He was taken away by Uncle Nikolai Yakovlev."

"Where to? Why?" the twins jumped up.

"Where, where, why should you care?" The father got upset. "Finish your meal and go to sleep!"

All grew silent. It was an understood family rule not to challenge Father. I was still too young to understand what had happened and was startled to see the tears in my brothers' eyes.

"But I know where Sharik is!" Petka suddenly blurted out. And no sooner had anyone's eye blinked when his next word glued each of us to our own seats, "Uncle Nikolai killed your Sharik with his gun."

Many years have passed, but I did not forget that moment. Dead silence first ensued and then the twins and I burst into tears. Looking at us, Petka also has begun to cry out with fright.

Mother quickly got up and went over to the stove, nervously shuffling things around. Babaka took Petka to the living room, whispering something in his ear.

Father, not looking at anyone, announced with a strong voice, "Nobody killed the dog! Uncle Nikolai Yakovlev found a person that needs a dog and took Sharik to him. He told me that the person is very good, loves dogs, and that your Sharik will have a good life there. So now, wipe away the snot and go to sleep! I don't want to hear any questions about that dog anymore!"

Tolka and Kolka frowned and darted away in the bedroom.

Night came. I could not fall asleep. My soul was childishly anxious and afraid. Everything was somehow wrong: scowling Father, his angry voice, the unhappy face of our mother, and sad, silent Babaka. But most importantly, Petka and his words. Maybe for the first time, my soul was truly troubled by something.

In the morning, when our parents went to work and Babaka left, the twins started asking Petka about Sharik. At first, he said nothing and looked at them through with fearful eyes. Kolka had promised to give him a ride on his bike, so Petka relented and led us outside. Between our house and neighboring houses, there was a small glade where we usually played soccer with an old rubber ball.

Petka led us there, and pointing, quickly blurted out, "Here is where Uncle shot Sharik with his gun. Sharik cried aloud and rolled over. Uncle shot again, and Sharik fell down. Then Uncle threw Sharik in his motorcycle and drove away."

Still not believing what we heard, we rushed over to the place to which Petka pointed and saw sand tangled here and there. Tolka raked away the sand with his foot, and we saw a big, dark red spot on the dirt.

"Blood! This is the blood of our Sharik!" screamed and wept Tolka. Tears streamed from my eyes, I turned and ran home. At home, I rushed to my bed and buried myself in the pillow and wept. My brothers were sobbing nearby. Nothing in the world could exceed the bitterness of those tears. We cried, not only from pity for Sharik, but even more out of resentment at the monstrous injustice and our powerlessness to change the tragedy that took place.

Babaka came, realizing what was the cause of our tears. She sat down on the old chest, and very softly, to no one in particular, began to speak, "We asked Uncle Nikolai to take Sharik to the hunting farm, where he works alone. But Sharik wouldn't allow him even to approach and then tore from his chain and ran. Uncle Nikolai tried to catch him, but Sharik attacked him and Uncle Nikolai was forced to shoot the dog."

"It's not true! It was all set up by our father!" Kolka cried through his tears and again buried his face in a pillow.

"Don't you dare talk like that about your father, small rascal!" Babaka warned him strictly. "He did his best! When you grow up, you will understand!"

For a long time, I could not forgive my father for Sharik's death. Having grown into an adult, I wanted to remind him of this sad story but did not know how to start the conversation. And then Father died. Grief erased both big and small resentments from my soul, leaving only the good memories. The story about the unusual history of our childhood pet, Sharik, was also forgotten, like many other even more dramatic stories, which have oddly served to shape my difficult life.

And here, in the dark basement of my cozy home in America, I came across a little volume of Asadov's poems, particularly his pure and naïve poem about a mutt. My heart was sweetly squeezed and my eyes grew moist. My poor, loyal Sharik! Pure of heart in the midst of a harsh and cruel time…

I was suddenly gripped with a simple realization. If it had not been for Sharik and his tragic ending, I do not know how my life would have been shaped in a different manner. The incredible devotion of that small "not of noble blood" mutt and the forced cruelty of adults deeply wounded my sensitive child's heart, causing it to tremble, worry, hate, and eventually... learn to forgive.

Had it not been for all of that, I might be a cruel person, unable to feel someone else's pain and suffering and would never possibly understood the passionate and selfless deed of the Human-God, who gave his life for us all on Golgotha.

Special thanks to Stephanie Starr and Alyssa Hart Blakemore, who helped me adjust my manuscripts to living, American English.

I also want to thank my brothers: Nikolai, Anatoli, and Peter; my sister, Vera; my sons: Roman, David; and daughter, Yelena; my grandkids: Nina and Dennis; Gail's parents: Corinne and Earl Wilson; my friends: Pavel Nurdin, Yakov Brauer, Nickolai Rozkaly, Alex Koval, Gary Mirzakhanov, Graeme Badger, John Hawk, James Sayler; my doctors: Keith Stampher and Brian Metz; my incredible students at UCCS and PPCC for their strong support of me during the hectic time I was writing this story.

My special gratitude is to the land of paradise, Hawaii, which inspired me to write the story about a person I really met there…